Stores of Winter

Marc Zimmerman

Global CASA Publications/Bravo y Allende Editores

Short Fiction

Bravo y Allende Editores

Authors Special First Edition

Stores of Winter.
Global CASA Publications and Bravo Allende Editores

Series in Literary Creation #2.

Published in Santiago, Chile. For information write Global CASA and LACASA Publications, Department of Modern and Classical Languages, University of Houston. 416 Agnes Arnold Hall. Houston, TX 77204-3006.

The author wishes to acknowledge the financial support of the GEAR (Grants to Enhance and Advance Research) of the University of Houston in developing and publishing this book.

"Valentine's Day, 1947" appeared first in *Descant*, XXIV, 10, 2 (Spring, 1979): 127-138; "The Landlord" appeared first in *Great River Review* 2, 2 (1980): 189-202.

Author's Special First Edition.

Zimmerman, Marc. 1939 –
Stores of Winter.
ISBN 0-9767019-4-4
1. Short Fiction
2. American Literature
3. Jewish American Literature

Cover drawing by Aaron Kerlow
Cover design by Flor Velásquez
Acknowledgements: Marino Segura for the Spanish;
Alessandro Carrera for the Italian.

"Ou sont les nieges . . . ?"

In memory of Dorothy and Bill.

Also for Elaine, Elmer, Adrienne,
Joanne, Samantha–
Esther and the Soler Family
Carlos, Jessie, A.C., G. and K.

Contents

THE TOURISTS

Part I.

1.

She lay in the hotel room waiting and hemorrhaging as he stepped off the curb and hailed the cab. –*¿Una farmacia?* –He said, hoping the cabdriver might understand his newly acquired Spanish to take him to a drugstore open this hour of the night.

–*¿Emergencia?* –he heard the driver ask. –*¡Sí!* –he answered. –*¡Sangre!* –he managed to say. He saw the cabdriver looking at him in the mirror, grimacing. He felt the car accelerate, jerkily, but still leaned forward, hoping to help the car along, half his mind in the hotel room with her, the other half subversively happy to be out in the night, entering the homes he passed, partaking of lives and loves very different from his own, entering these lives even if only in imagination, perhaps happy too that it was no more than this. *He stumbled down a row of beds, climbing finally into one, and finding, of course to his surprise, that it was not empty.* The cabdriver, fat and stocky, his weight sinking him down in the seat of his aging grey Seat, began to talk in incomprehensible torrents, nervous cascades of words (were they aphorisms?) as his mission lured them further out into the night, past one closed drugstore after another, they riding through unknown neighborhoods, she bleeding, waiting for his success and return.

2.

The "emergency" had begun after their days in Port Bou, in Gerona, Barcelona, Castellón de La Plana and Valencia, and even after a week walking the streets of Madrid, loaded down with their discount tipping guidebook and their Hemmingway stories, seeking out the story settings, staying even in the hotel where the busboy was impaled on knives tied to the legs of a chair. The weather had turned raw, cold; even as the guide book impelled them toward ever cheaper bargains; it became clearer that the book only worked in the summer when there was no problem with coldwater rooms, broken windows and threadbare blankets. But they doggedly kept to the code, relentlessly sought to break new records—innocents abroad, as he would learn to define them years later.

But really with all the growing weather problems, the "emergency" had not begun for certain until they had endured the cold budget hotels and wind torn streets of Toledo; and then (it was at his insistence to be sure, but wasn't he merely trying to impress her with his evermore rigorous pursuit of a logic she had taught him?) he had refused to travel back to Madrid as the better way to go (better to pick up a first class bus from the capital city to Seville), but instead proudly found an almost unheard of local bus to take them down through the Spanish plain to the town of Ciudad Real, where they would find a room and ready themselves to board a train that would leave early the next morning on a route leading to Cordoba.

The Toledo cold had been truly miserable, and their compulsion to visit every church, synagogue and shop in the guidebook on those raw December days had probably set them up for the worst. The crude hotel rooms only kept them to the streets all the more. They might have been barely adequate for the spring or summer, but at this time of year, without heat and with blankets unable to keep out the cold, they could not have been more inhospitable.

At the root of the problem had been their obsession with saving money. Life was travel and adventure. But you needed cash. Money gave you time, travel, adventure—life itself. But you had to watch your money, hold it back. Each slip, each error cost you days, cost you time, so you would have to end travel, end life, to work and save so that you could travel and live again. So they had waited to travel off-season, and struggled each day to find a cheaper restaurant, a cheaper hotel, a slightly better discount on a museum or train as the days grew colder and shorter.

Why, after all, go back to Madrid, search around for still another hotel (for their general rule of adventure was automatically and almost dogmatically "something new")—only to end up having to repeat a journey out, to begin once again in the same direction south. Her goal, after all, was to see as much of Europe as possible on their limited resources. Who had in fact visited Ciudad Real? Wasn't the city mentioned in Lope de Vega's most famous play? And wasn't it *novel* to go there? So why go back, or why even stay an extra night in Toledo, and wait for the (admittedly) more frequent and varied morning transportation when they could exhaust (and check off) their guidebook listings by early morning, have a last lunch, return to see that El Greco in the church one more time (because that return trip did make cultural sense), and still have time to take the leisurely (and special) great late afternoon bus trip he had discovered (perhaps the first American?) in a timetable his hotel was using to pad the window—a trip to a place which they might otherwise never chance to visit in their lives.

And so it was they waited in the Church staring at the luminous "El Greco" painting of some solemn symbolic funeral, shivering and waiting for the time to take the bus. And so it was that they waited in the bus station for almost an hour after the bus was scheduled to leave, as the driver waited without passion and almost without expression for his cousin's girlfriend to show up with the two hens that she was taking to her aunt. - *But why can't we at least wait on the bus?* - asked the American.

A black-toothed worker shrugged and offered him a cigarette. –*La meme chose en Allemagne* –he said, winking. Clearly a returning guest worker mocking the northern reputation for punctuality, he decided, or mocking foreign tourists, it occurred to him on second thought. Finally the girl and her hens arrived and every one piled onto the bus. With a cough and a spurt, it sputtered and jerked its way out of the city, down the hill of Toledo and into the countryside, proceeding to meander through the gold-turned hills and past the Civil War grave markers of the Castilian plateau in the late afternoon and twilight. –*¡Los cabrones!* –he heard the worker whisper, and they turned to see him sitting right behind them. –*He means they're all fascist graves* -whispered a Spaniard speaking English with a quite Londonish, almost cockney accent. He could not help but squirm nervously, nodding at the two men, but feeling his shoulders rise, wishing they would be more silent, And why had it not occurred to him before that he and his wife might not be the only ones who spoke English on that quaint local bus that plunged and lurched and wound its way southward down the Castilian plain in what was already the twenty-fifth year of peace in Spain?

3.

–*¡Me cago en la mierda!* –the taxi driver exclaimed, spitting out his window. He had stopped twice now at drugstores the list he had said were supposed to be open. –*¡Tendremos que ir a la Triana!* –he said slowly so the American might be able to follow. –*La...* –he repeated. –*¡Sí, sí!* –he insisted. Place of guitars and castanets and gypsies. Streets of thieves, he had been there already, seen a *tablao.* But going there now was different.

The driver weaved through streets that seemed ever narrower, then crossed a bridge, thread his way through streets the American had never seen before. Even at this hour, when the bars were supposed to be closed, he could catch the sounds of music coming from the cabarets, and occasionally he spotted wavering silhouettes in windows and doorways, couples dancing or embracing, drunks propping themselves up against walls. –*I suppose they're not really whorehouses* –he mused, thinking of the tight pseudo-Catholic official morality of the dictatorship. – *¡Aquí no se puede!* –the cabbie sang out, more to himself than to his customer.

– *¡Pero aquí se tiene que...! ¿Qué?* –he repeated, not understanding a word. –*¡Dinero!*–said the cabdriver, and to make his point, he pulled a professional wad from his pocket, and waved it back and forth. –*¡Mucho!* –the cabdriver said. –*¡Sí, sí!* –he replied, understanding. *¡Dinero! ¡Pago! ¡Sí!* –he said, trying to make it clear that he was ready to pay whatever it might take.

Of course he was willing to pay, he had to—even if it meant violating the tourism contract: pay and pay all that was necessary at last, without trying to cut corners. She had been bleeding, not heavily, not (he thought) so dangerously, but it was like an eternal period, in the flow and the pains and moods she suffered. And he felt useful to be on this mission, happy to be away from her too, happy to be away and with a justifying excuse, happy to have bases for reverie and fantasy based on all that had happened to him and all he had wanted to happen that hadn't, happy to imagine possibilities even if he knew he would do nothing to make them materialize. And he dug into his pocket for his wallet, pulled it out and checked to see if he had enough "pesetas" for his mission, and then for his fantasy adventures. –*Enough to open closed doors* –he thought, –*to buy what was needed, yes and to dance and more.*

–*But damn! Ciudad* Real *cost a lot!* –he thought, as the cab wheeled around a corner and entered a dark section of Triana he had never seen. –*And it's still costing* –he told himself, still counting the strange and dirty bills as best he could, when the driver stopped short and began blowing his horn, calling: *–¡Pepe!¡Pepe!* As lights went on in all the apartments and people began staring out their windows, some of them catcalling at the driver, one even throwing an empty can which just missed the car and clattered down the cobbled street.

4.

Well, and how was he to know that the bus would leave so late, that the Ciudad Real bus depot was on the outskirts of town and not in the center, and that there was only one cab, and that they would be among the last to get it as it made its trips to and from the station. They arrived at the depot at seven, but it took them another hour to get into town. From the main square, they tried all the budget hotels, and at each were told that there was no room, but they should try the next one down the street. Soon all the recommendations pointed to hotels already visited. And it was clear there was no regular room available, they carting their handful of luggage around the square and onto side-streets, once sitting down to warm and rest themselves in a cafe, drinking glasses of "El Presidente" (at only six pesetas a shot, she had pointed out when they'd had their first drink in Port Bou), to get a second wind and decide what they could do.

Her Spanish better than his, she asked the waiter: *–¿Hay habitaciones? Los hoteles en la plaza son llenos.* Then he turned to the bartender and they discussed the matter. Neither waiter nor barman seemed to know what to say. They shrugged at each other, grunted out some words that seemed rebuking, as if each attacked the other's ignorance and inability to help. But after all it wasn't their problem. *–No. Perdón, señores, es que no sabemos* –said the waiter *–si los hoteles están repletos. No hay cuartos.* And then he stopped, stepped back toward the bartender and conferred once again, this time both of them nodding as if they had resolved the problem. They gestured them to the door, and pointed down the street to an office on which they could see the insignia of the Spanish Government, and even a shingle with letters large enough so they could make them out from where they stood: "Oficina de turismo." The government campaign of going all out for tourists seemed to work after all. Thanking the waiter and paying, they made their way to the office, their problem all but solved, approaching with great anticipation, the twilight coming on and icy rain falling ever more harshly as a raw wind seemed to rise, arriving at the office, only to find a sign on the door, one not readable from the restaurant but that close up was especially elegant, replete with a silhouette of the young Franco and with impeccable lettering which spelled out the dreaded word: "*cerrado*."

5.

Finally an aproned woman came out of one of the houses and onto the street, and greeted the cabbie like an old friend. The woman he surmised was the cabbie's cousin turned and shook his hand and then gestured for them both to wait as she made her way back into the building and up the stairs. Some minutes later, she came out of the house, this time with a man who, half asleep or drunk, grunted and spat his way over to them, all the while struggling to tuck his shirt into his pants. He and the cabbie embraced, then motioned to the woman to climb in the cab and for them all to follow after him, as he made his way down the street. –*Must be her husband*–he thought, keeping score on kinship ties. And maybe he owns a drugstore. Sure enough, they came finally to a store clearly marked "Farmacia." The cousin's husband gestured for them to wait, as he pulled out a set of keys, fumbled for the right one and finally opened the gate and door which led into the store. They were about to follow, when he mumbled that they should wait. And wait they did, the wife trying to explain something to the cabdriver, who simply shrugged in the American's direction. Finally, it was she who indicated that they could now enter, leading them through the door to face the counter behind which, now appearing very much the keeper of his business, standing amidst his sparse provisions, the husband patiently and pleasantly awaited them. –*¿Y qué le puedo ofrecer*? –he asked.

The latter fumbled through his pockets until he found the note his wife had written for him and which he now read, utilizing the pronunciation she had taught him: –*¿Hay mee dol y tampax*?–he asked.

6.

They stared at the sign and closed office, peering in the doorway, trying to imagine what they would have found out, what excellent service they would have received had they been able to enter the office earlier. And now, for the first time in all this mounting misadventure, she glared at him, fully. Without her saying a word, he knew she blamed it all on him, everything on him, as if there could be no question of her complicity, no question of her having made no contribution to the situation they now found themselves in, other than having made the stupid and improbable but not irreversible choice, of course, of having married him and suggesting this trip in the first place. Never having fully wanted to go, fearful of everything in life, insecure, quite younger than she and no match for her in will, he simply, once having agreed to the trip, had doggedly followed out the logic she had insisted on giving it. And what else was he supposed to have done when countering her only led to deeper conflicts until he finally gave in? He glared back at her bitterly, searched her long black hair, once so short, hoping to find at least one white hair. He found none and found himself turning to the young Franco silhouette smiling from the sign.

She started off down the street, and he plunged after her, putting his hand under her arm, lugging their bags as a gust of wind raced at their faces. Suddenly he saw the almost-cockney speaking Spaniard who had sat with the black-toothed worker on the bus. –*No luck finding a room?* –he said, approaching them. –*No luck at all*–she answered for both of them.

–*Miren, señores...* A burly Spaniard suddenly lurched out of a doorway; his face scarred around one eye, both eyes reddened from years of much drinking. And without a word he took up the suitcases he had dropped to speak to the English-speaking traveler. Took one up with his left hand and braced another with an arm which he suddenly saw was amputated, as he stared at what was no more than a stump covered by clotted rags. –*A veteran* –the almost-cockney whispered, exchanging glances with the couple, and urging them to come along, which they did, simply and humbly following their self-appointed guide and savior down through the streets of Ciudad Real. The hard rain kept on, at times turning to ice, as they marched up one street, down another, and the streets grew ever narrower. –*¡Ahí!* –their guide finally said, pointing to a rundown old house, perhaps where Lope himself might have stayed if he had conducted local research about the area and the god-forsaken city for his play.

7.

The cab ride back seemed so fast. He clutched his purchases in his hand, feeling satisfied, drawing on the bitter tobacco the cabbie gave him. The car pulled up to the hotel. He paid the cabbie a big fee and generous tip, shook his hand, sighed, and then saw him off before making his way into the hotel past the reception area and up the staircase.

He hesitated before the door to their room, opening the door ever so slowly, only to find her naked on the bed with tee shirts of his twisted together forming a white mass to sop up the blood. She crying, looking at him bitterly, her eyes peering through her long black hair that all but covered her face, he trying to forget all the times she'd fooled and abandoned him, her vagaries and infidelities, the petty and deep flung insults to his fragile sense of being, his ever so tentative creative will. She most vulnerable now through that part of herself she most resented. He a crazed incompetent who had ventured into the night and risked traffic with gypsies and thieves and whores to bring back to his lady love... (this being Seville of this time) kotex and aspirin he had been compelled to settle for in the drugstore in la Triana.

8.

The building was not a hotel, but, it seemed, a place for poor itinerant salesmen, traveling low level officials, migratory workers even old-style religious pilgrims, mendicants, drunks, moors, Arabs, perhaps even lepers, in short, every sort of transient the traffic would allow. A stern, nun like woman, straight and plain, with the faintest moustache shadow to give her a suggestion of character, took them through a common room full of beds where already several men and just a few women were preparing themselves for the night. –*Es todo lo que puedo ofrecer* –she said gruffly to the cockney-speaking Spaniard, pointing to a rumpled bed. He shrugged good naturedly, dumped his bag on the bed and dismissed them with a friendly wave. –*Supongo que no son maricas.* –he said, gesturing to the men around him. The woman glared at him a moment, but the men in ear's range said nothing. – *No querer here.* –he told them, as the woman led them on past a snoring gypsy, out of the common room, into a small chamber with two cots, bed pan for night pissing, a pitcher and a wash basin. –*Home*–he said to his wife. –*Mi casa es tu casa.* The woman gave them the meanest stare, as if to say they were quite welcome to spend the night in the street for all she cared.

But it was clear this was home for the night. He paid her the hundred pesetas on the spot, and waited for her to leave. Then she glared at him and he said nothing, looking toward the door, and toward their almost-cockney-speaking friend, only to see him huddled on the edge of his bed with the one-armed guide, sharing a bottle together, acting all so chummy, and even (was he hearing right?) and laughing together.

9.

–*¡Pero, señor! ¡No tenemos tales productos norteamericanos! Somos gente pobre y tradicionalista aquí en España*– said the druggist. –*Pobres, pero decentes, y esos productos…, quién sabe.* It had all started with him trying to explain what these strange products were. Now the cabbie's cousin had gotten into it, crossing herself and making much tongue-clicking, head-turning "todo", as the discussion rattled on, at times seeming to verge on violence, as if a single misguided word or gesture could tip the already loaded scale. The cabbie kept trying to intervene, trying to explain and straighten things out, and the scene seemed to grow hotter almost in proportion to his efforts at clarification and peacemaking. It was simply clear to him that these products were not yet known in Spain, that yes, perhaps in the Madrid Hilton, one might be able to find them, but not in Seville, and certainly not in "la Triana." So yes, he should be happy to get away without a black eye or a knife in the gut, and yes, he would have to make do, and yes, pay a good price for the making as well.

10.

They had found a place to sleep, but by the time they had eaten and wandered down to the train station where they bought the tickets to leave at dawn, the night had turned bitterly cold, and when they returned to the room, it was freezing. She began tearing up old newspapers to pad the tall windows inch by inch, while he sought out the "mustached señora" to get an extra blanket.

But he could find her nowhere and began walking up and down the rows of the common sleeping room, filled with the low grind of snores and wheezes, an occasional belch or stomach growl, maybe a pittling fart. He looked everywhere for a blanket, maybe one that had fallen off one of the sleepers, even approaching his fellow-traveler, only to see him curled up blissfully snoring away, his one-armed veteran friend no where to be seen.

All the beds filled, no extra blankets to be had, he came back to the room empty-handed. By now she had padded the window and even taped down a crack in one of the window panes. But the cold seemed worse than ever. They took the bedding off the first cot and tucked it all neatly on the second. They opened their suitcase and found some dirty clothes they used to pad their pants and sweaters. Finally they crawled under the thin blankets and held each other in the narrow cot, embracing more fully than in months, without the slightest trace of affection, but only out of self-protective need.

11.

She sat up, glaring and shaking with pain. –*You son of a bitch*! –She said, –*You useless, self-important bastard I was stupid enough to marry—big hotshot off in a cab and look what you've brought me. I'm bleeding to death. And all because you're a cheap bastard who's ruined my life just to save a few miserable pesetas.*

Part II.

1.

It seemed to him they had hardly slept, but somehow they must have, because how else could they have awakened? The water in the basin was frozen so hard he could not break through to find liquid for washing. As they packed and closed their suitcases, their breath formed clouds before them. They trudged their way past the sleeping transients, out the door and into the square, retracing the steps to the train station just as they had rehearsed it all the night before. The cold rain kept falling on them as they moved bitterly through the streets, finally arriving at the station. Their almost-cockney-speaking fellow traveler was already there and nodded grimly toward them. They moved to the other extreme of the station.

It seemed interminable before the train came, the cold so cutting, the train so slow in coming, so long in waiting at the station and departing. Only third class seats were left, so they sat on frozen benches, savoring old class distinctions still alive in the now modernizing regime, as their train made its way ever so slowly south off the Castilian plain and on to Cordoba.

2.

And it was truly bad in the famous city. They walked about seeking out the old Arab and Jewish buildings, zebra-striped arches and mosques. But it threatened rain and rained, the damp air penetrating to the bone. She began to grow feverish, sweating even in the cold. He walked her back to their hotel, protective, cuddling her as they ambled through rain and puddles, helping her up the stairs to their room, their bed, helping her off with her clothes, getting her under the covers, and then going downstairs once again to the little restaurant off the lobby, to order hot tea and some toast.

When he returned, she was already asleep. He lay beside her and watched the beads of sweat form on her face. He fell asleep only to wake to dampness on his thigh and a familiar acrid smell in his nostrils. –*Her period!*–he said to himself, examining the bedding. –*Your period*–he replied seeing her turn toward him. –*I just had one a week ago.* –she mumbled, turning away and returning to sleep.

3.

It was hard to get any one to listen. The soccer games had begun in Latin America and blared on every radio throughout early December, the men sitting around the TV sets, watching every game. All he could make out was "goal," and that was rare enough. Stupid game of frustrated moves, broken strategies, problem solving and failure...! Only in truly foreign places could they like that litany of dashed hopes and broken dreams!

They would go out for awhile, at least at first. But the rain felt cold and harsh. Every place seemed damp. The bleeding kept on day after day, five days now, and it was beginning to seem like an eternal period, with cramps and irritation, sometimes hysteria, the hysteria mounting with a growing inarticulate fear of what it all was. And there were no doctors who spoke English, so why bother? A call to the Consulate only confirmed it. –*Wait and see a few days*–he was advised –*and if the bleeding doesn't stop, go on to Seville.*

The games kept on, day after day, one after another. The rain kept on day after day. So did the bleeding. Stupid games, miserable weather, fucked up life. It was time to move on to Seville.

4.

The trip and hotel search left her absolutely drained, almost without the strength to stand. He found them a decent enough hotel, more comfortable and expensive than their norm, but respectful both of her illness and their still existing if unwritten contract for the trip. As soon as they entered the room, she collapsed on the bed and fell into a heavy sleep. He went outside, lingered in the twilight, marveling at the warmer weather and the promise of tomorrow's sun which the last rays of daylight seemed to make. He walked around the neighborhood of curved narrow streets, taking in here the way he had imagined all of Spain to be: the tile roofs, the patios, the passageways, the whiteness. That evening he brought her a light meal from the small hotel restaurant; and when she fell back to sleep, he returned to the dinning room, where the wife of the hotel owner helped him find the number and address of the American consulate, in case he might need it.

But the next day, the bleeding had stopped. –*Thank God, it's over.* –she said. But she seemed weaker than ever before. She insisted on going out and seeing the city and wouldn't listen to his urgings that she wait a few days. When he spoke of going to the Consulate to get the names of the English-speaking doctors they were sure to find here, she insisted that no, the illness was over and since it was over once and for all, there was no need to find out what it might have been. They wandered around the town, entering *La Casa de las Indias*, one and another church, when suddenly she grew so weak that she could hardly sit up on the park bench he had led her to. He hailed a cab and got them back to the hotel, impatiently taking the room key off the lobby counter and hurrying her to their room, where she could lie down. Once she was undressed and asleep, he went to the lobby and asked directions for the Consul's office. But the manager saved him the trip by phoning ahead. He came up with the names and numbers of three doctors. Two of them were not considered much, but the third helped in emergencies at the large hotels where the Americans stayed. He was supposed to be a fine person, a reliable practitioner, a man with lots of connections and influence.

And so it was that the doctor was chosen. The hotel clerk called and made the appointment for the next day. He then carefully explained to him how they were to get there. Then the soccer game came on. The clerk's friends turned away, as he continued to study the maps and routes. Through the window he saw the sun cloud over, saw the sky darken, and the rain begin to fall. Years later he would remember those days in Seville as ones without sun and with rain falling without letup for ten days.

In the end they took a cab, finally stopping at a wrought iron gate with a plaque marked, "Dr. José Antonio Sánchez-Baraciega. Se habla inglés." Framing the gate portal and extending the complete length of the fence which fronted the house was an elaborate relief presenting an allegory of sin and good and God, with barking three-headed dogs, wanton, diseased-scarred women, horrendously twisted cripples, some seeming lepers, dwarves and gnomes, and, walking among all these creatures, a Christ, bloodied and crucified, attempting, through all his pain, to sanctify the hellish scene. They had no choice but to risk the realms of hell, making their way up the walk to the front door and entering a waiting room, where a ruddy old man, apparently more porter than receptionist, grunted a hello and bade them to sit down on a red-leather couch, and handed them a form to be filled out. Was it a matter of amusing themselves until the doctor was ready to see them, or was it a test of their eligibility for service? The form seemed incredibly complicated, filled with technical questions featuring a specialized vocabulary that might stymie even a native user of the language. Meanwhile, the old man shuffled off to the next room, apparently to alert the doctor that he had people waiting. He felt uneasy that there were no other patients, and the uneasiness grew when the old man returned, and he noticed (why was he always so slow in seeing?) that the man only had one arm. —*Another Civil War vet.* —he thought.

Finally the doctor himself (clearly the doctor: tallish, paunchy, slightly balding, with every gesture indicating this to be his place) opened the door to the inner office and motioned for them to come in. —*¿Usted habla inglés?* –his wife began. —*Sí.* –he answered, motioning toward the diplomas on his wall, including one from an obscure, almost unheard of school in Kansas. —*Bueno,* –she said, looking relieved, stumbling, stammering —*Estoy enferma, estoy con sangre, es... siempre.* —*Sí.* –he nodded, motioning for her to come over to his examination area, behind a screen. And when they paused, he snapped on a pair of plastic gloves and impatiently motioned once again. She looked at the two men with alarm and the beginnings of outrage. At home a male doctor would generally have a woman present during such an exam. —*You have a nurse?* – she said weakly. —*¡No, no!* –he said with surprising firmness. Apparently this was doctor's work and there would be no concessions. He was probably insulted just by her suggestion and show of anxiousness. She resigned herself and so did he. A flow of communication simply had not developed, and the doctor had made them unwilling participants in his version of the national game of facing-down. Really, what other choice did they have? She followed the doctor back behind the screen. He tried to follow, but the doctor stopped him. —*¡No!* –he said with the same firmness, physically stopping him and urging him back. —*¡Okay! ¡Okay!* –he added, apparently by way of reassurance. —*¡Okay!* –he answered, shrugging his shoulders.

When they emerged, she had a soured, pained look. The doctor looked pensive. —*Bueno, me...* –he started, —*¡En inglés, por favor!* –she asked —*That's why we came to you!* The doctor continued, —*Yes, yes. Infección.* –he said, taking off his bloodied gloves. —*Infection, that is* –he repeated in English. —*A cold* –he said, as if to explain, dumping the gloves into a sink. —*No worry! A cold!* –he replied, repeating but not comprehending. —*In the uterine wall?* –she asked. —*A cold! Not serious!* –the Dr. repeated, scrawling out what must have been a prescription. —*She will be all right? Yes! Every day this medicine.* –he said to her, playing father, —*Make you sleepy, mareada, ¿cómo se dice?* —*Nauseous?* –she offered. —*Yes* –he repeated, *mareada, nauseous* – smiling and tucking his prescription into her hand. —*You get better ... in week. Si no, you come back. ... Very pretty* –he assured the American, patting her on the cheek. —*Pretty woman... Mexican?* –he asked. —*Italiana* –she told him, glaring, —*Italian-American.* —*Ah* –he said —*very pretty. Mangano, Lolabrigida, Magnani, Loren, Vitti, very pretty, pretty-pretty. Good-looking ladies... How you say? Real sexy, no? ... You pay el señor, ¿ no?*

He escorted them to the door, and as he ushered them out, the American glanced over the doctor's desk, again saw the certificates from here, there and everywhere, and for the first time noticed, over the doctor's plush couch, photos of John Kennedy and Franco, the two heroes, smiling down on the scene. Then in the waiting room, as he paid the old veteran, he noticed (again for the first time) a picture on the wall of an ever so saintly and pure Christ looking down on his fallen mockers and crucifiers, with pained, compassionate and forgiving eyes as infernal pitchfork-toting little demons prodded them off to their flame-lit fate.

5.

They filled the prescription at the pharmacy near the hotel, but not without incident. The pharmacist took Sánchez-Bariciega's note and stared at it for some time. Then he handed it to his wife at the cash-register. They both shrugged their shoulders, exchanging bewildered glances. —*Sánchez-Baraciega* –the man said, as if asking. —*¡Sí!* –he answered. Then the pharmacist shrugged his shoulders again. —*¿Qué tiene de mal, señora?* —*Catarro* –she said. —*¿Pero ahí?* –he asked, apparently astounded. —*¡Médicos!* –the pharmacist's wife said, smiling cheerfully at the couple, as her husband shrugged his shoulders once again, and turned to make up the order.

6.

She took the medicine three times a day every day after day as the rain kept falling and the Spanish men watched game after game of soccer. She insisted on venturing out with him, taking in the sights, going to a few stores to watch the Christmas shopping, both of them conscious of their accelerating expenses, and the fact that they could not buy anything until they knew where her illness was going and where it would take them.

The bleeding ebbed and flowed, but did not stop. With the flow came the tension and delirium, which mounted daily. She told him how she dreamed of blood, of heavy rains and seas of blood, of herself drowning in red torrents, of women, beautiful women, gagging, choking and drowning in the bloody waves that broke over them. And she dreamt too of the doctor, putting on his plastic gloves and probing her vagina, his smiling face blending with Franco's and Kennedy's. She would awaken sweating, glaring at him. Sometimes she dug her fingernails into his shoulder or side, digging until he cried out with pain. Sometimes they lay in bed staring at each other, without touching, They both trembled, thinking of cancer.

Soon it was clear the medicine was not working. They had their hotel clerk call for another appointment, only to find that the doctor was on vacation "en Canarias," the one-armed veteran reported. With our money and the money of other suckers, he could not help but think bitterly. He himself dreamed, —*No worry, no worry* –said Dr. Sánchez-Baraciega, smiling, but somehow there was dirt or some other brown substance seeping through his teeth and onto his lips and chin. Then he felt her shaking him. "*Cancer!*" she yelled into his face. "*I'm dying of cancer and all you do is sitting around telling me not to worry.*" She looked at him and began to cry. —*She needs me to do something special* –he thought, and he knew he had to do something, or at least get out of the room, because he suddenly felt he would suffocate. —*And I'm all out of tampax* –she said, crying like a baby. —*And my head hurts so much, and—Maybe it's the medicine that's killing her* –he thought, —*or Spain.* That's when he went out into the night and found his "Rocinante" Seat and went off to "la Triana."

7.

But nothing worked, the doctor gone, the city paralyzed in rain and soccer games. The night after his failed night mission, she awoke in deep pain. The aspirin only hurt her more. On the mattress there was a veritable pool. When he tried to speak to her, she just turned away, sobbing, hitting her fists against the pillow. He tried to talk again, overwhelmed by guilt and helplessness. —*For god's sake*, –she said finally —*don't let me die in this hotel. Christ, for once in your life, do something!*

8.

He walked out on the street, not knowing which way to turn, walking aimlessly at first, up one street, down another in the barrio. He thought of going to the American consulate. He envisioned a quick rescue. (After all, he was American; they were duty-bound to help, to ship them to the U.S. and solve all their problems). And suddenly he stopped, appalled by his own fantasy. —*What a Yankee doodle dandy I am!* –he said to himself in disgust. And he realized that part of the fantasy was merely a wish to get out of this damned country, to get out of Europe and back to somewhere where the ground was firm and sure: home in California. But he knew the contracted code was still in place: It was his job to find a solution here in Europe, and it was his job to see that the solution was inexpensive and helped spur on their wonderful journey: free-souled Americans on the road.

But how accomplish all this? He continued walking through the streets, stopping in plazas, staring at fountains in the rain. Then he passed a door with a posted sign: "ginecólogo." On other walks he had seen such signs—there were many of them. But the clerk had told him they weren't really M.D.'s, they were more like "parteras"—high-class midwives. Not reliable, not for modern Americans like him and his wife. But couldn't they help? Standing before this particular one, he convinced himself that it was more affluent-looking than usual. A wealthy one's probably a successful one, he thought. He hesitated for a moment, trying to think of how he should present the case, how he should get this man to come to his aid and rescue them, strangers in a foreign land. But then he could think of nothing, and decided to act on impulse and instinct. So he went up the walk and entered the office.

The small waiting room was crammed with women, many accompanied by children, some by mothers, a few by husbands. Clearly the wait would be a long one, he realized, as a nurse urged him to take a chair, fill out some forms and wait his turn.

He decided not to wait. He scribbled a note in big letters and handed it to the nurse as she was helping one of the women to fill out the form. —*¡Por favor!* –he said —*¡Por favor!* The woman read the note and stared at him intently. —*¡Por favor!* –he repeated, and she left the room immediately. A second later, the doctor came out, a young man moving quickly—efficient, but clearly concerned and alerted.

In that instant, he shouted at the doctor precisely what he had scrawled on the paper: *¡Sangre! ¡Mucha sangre! ¡Esposa…! ¡Sangre!*

Several of the women jumped to their feet, looking this way and that, as if expecting to see his bloody wife stagger in the door, perhaps a knife in her ribs, her entrails oozing to the floor—or perhaps they expected to see her bloodied and bludgeoned body materialize itself someplace in the office.

The young doctor acted with controlled fury. —*¡Cálmese!*–he said firmly, taking him by the shoulder and luring him into his office.

9.

As best he could, and with the doctor's patient help, he explained what had happened and what was happening to his wife, the nature of her illness, the strain she'd been under. He used gestures, broken phrases, pantomime, and it seemed he was being understood. Above all, he stressed the need for a doctor who could communicate, one who could speak enough English to really explain what she had and what had to be done. —*In inglés*–he heard himself repeating, —*inglés* y *sangre: no no sa… sangre*–he stammered. —*Sí*–the doctor said, nodding his head to indicate he more or less understood what he was being told. —*Inglés, ¡como en Ingleterra, Gilbraltar! ¡Sí!*–he echoed the doctor, "¡*Inglés*!" like a prayer.

The doctor gestured for even more patience and less anguish. –*No worry*–he said, but somehow it didn't sound or feel sinister. Already he grew more confident and hopeful. —*He's going to give me the name of some one,*–he thought, —*some one who's very much like him, who maybe even looks like him, maybe his brother even, (if only this man could speak English!), but some one who could fill the bill.* —*No sé*–the doctor said, and he took out his pen and wrote out the name and telephone number he was sure would help the American. Taking the piece of paper, the American thanked the doctor with a sense of gratitude that felt absolutely boundless. He looked the doctor straight in his eyes, hoping to memorize the moment forever. But the mood collapsed and vanished as he unfolded the paper and read:

"Dr. José Antonio Sánchez-Baraciega
Se habla inglés."

Suddenly the weight of defeat seemed to enter his pores and then his veins. His legs weakened, his stomach sank. —*Gracias*–he said futilely, his head dipping downward. —*Muchas* –he said, turning toward the door and leaving, his entire body feeling more leaden by the second.

10.

On his way back to the hotel, he passed by a large schoolyard. In an instant, he saw some students racing across the grounds, carrying banners he could not read and screaming words he couldn't understand. A second later, several mounted police went charging by on horseback, chasing down the students, clubbing them down and trampling a few. –*¡Fuera!*–a mounted cop snapped at him, the horse whinnying, blood coming from his mouth around the bit which was clearly digging in. "*Usted*" was the only other word he heard and understood.

11.

He reached the hotel and went up to their room. The shutters were drawn. He could see nothing. Then suddenly his eyes adjusted as the sound of harsh breathing reached his ears and the reek of blood reached his nostrils. Reddened kotex lay strewn all about. Large red stains crisscrossed on white walls and even on the ceiling. The large standing clothes rack was open, the mirror facing out, showing him his own eyes and gaping mouth growing wider by the second. Then he heard bitter, wrenching sobs. He shoved over the mirror door and there she was squatting on the seat of a chair, stark naked, her face and body smeared with blood, streams of toilet paper at her feet, and on the floor around the chair.

My god, –he groaned —*what's happening?* —*You bastard!* –she said —*Dirty bastard! You want to kill me; you've been killing ever since we met!* –she sobbed and whined, glaring at him. *Calm down*, was all he could think of saying. —*Calm down, no worry!*–she answered, mocking him and Baraciega at once, —*Don't say talk to me, you jerk off son of a bitch!* He put his arm on hers to stop her. But she began gashing him with her nails. She dug into his back and sides, and then went to his cheek and began to rip at them, reaching for his eyes, gouging his nose.

At that point he let her have it. He grabbed her hair and pushed her away, and when she dug her nails into his right arm, he slapped her violently with the left. And when she slammed him back to the head, he hit her to the stomach. And when she kicked at his groin, he kicked her right back in her bleeding crotch.

—*Oh!* –she shrieked, holding herself and stumbling forward toward the bed, looking at him in amazement, groaning. For the first time, he heard noises in the hall and some one pounding on the door. —*¡Qué pasa!* –the owner screamed in anger. He opened the door only to be greeted by a piece of used kotex which she hurled in his face. —*Leave me alone!* –she cried, —*Leave me fucking alone!* –The owner closed the door, but shouted in outrage the key word of the hour: —*¡Fuera, fuera!*

12.

—*We have to get out of here!* –he told her, face in his hands, stunned by what he had done. —*But where, where can we go?* –she asked. *Ciudad Real? Or, I know. Why don't we go back to Toledo and start all over? Of course we could go to Ciudad Real, or we could go to Cordoba...*

—*No,* –he said suddenly with an idea. She sobbed bitterly, —*Why did I have to bleed? What did I do to myself, marrying with some one so useless and nothing. A man—that's bad enough. And a man like you, ha!* –she sobbed, oblivious to his bright idea, still bending over, lamenting and cursing him. And he realized the Fascist cop and the hotel owner had pointed to the solution that the doctor mid-wife had indeed given him after all. —*Gibraltar,* –he said —*fucking Gibraltar!*

Part III.

1.

He transferred their things to another hotel for the night, then arranged their trip to the coast and checked them out of the hotel, avoiding the glare of the owner's outraged eyes as he paid their bill and brushed her past the front desk and out the door forever.

They made the move hardly without a word beyond the most necessary logistical matters, and they slept in the separate beds he had specifically requested, avoiding any contact of body or eye.

Again without words or touching, they traveled all the next day, taking a bus to Algeciras and then another to La Línea de la Concepción, checking into a hotel where she rested while he crossed the border into Gibraltar and sought out an appropriate doctor to discuss her problems and make an appointment. Inquires along the business street led him to a Dr. Johnson, chief gynecologist of the hospital. —*Can I help you?* –she asked when he entered her office.

2.

The next day they crossed the border together and went to Dr. Johnson's office. —*She has a low grade vaginal infection.* –she said, studying the test results. It seemed the medicine Baraciega had prescribed was the worst kind of stuff, apt to induce systemic imbalances that brought on hysteria and further hemorrhaging. Now there was no help for it. –*She needs to throw away that Sevillan witch brew and have a D. and C. as soon as possible,* –she said. Everything was quickly arranged for her to enter the hospital the next day for an operation and recovery period that would cost them roughly $33.50. —*Three cheers for British chauvinism, socialism and imperialism,* –he thought.

3.

They went back to sleep in La Línea, still not talking, still tense, but much relieved by having something focused to deal with. That night, Christmas players paraded the streets singing and playing exotic, Arab-sounding songs. A *Falangista* contingent roamed in bands weaving in and out of the parading singers, carrying placards and chanting slogans that called for the British to leave Gibraltar. "*Fuera,*" the signs read and people called, *¡fuera!*. That very night La Linea's radio station carried a speech by *el Caudillo* denouncing British occupation of Spanish territory. She lay sedated in the room, and he went out, wandered among the parading crowd, and then went to the local movie theater to see *Franco, Ese Hombre*, a tribute to the great spokesman for national sovereignty.

Afterwards, from the balcony, he went back to watching the street singers and demonstrating "falangistas", who were still at it and seemed set to keep up their doings the whole night through. One excited woman addressed the people with a bull-horn. —*The British must leave!* –he understood her to say. —*Not for another week*. –he prayed.

4.

He booked her into the hospital, still hardly without a word between them, and found they would not operate until the next day. He made his way back to the border, happy to be alone and hoping to maintain his Spanish residence because of the much lower hotel costs. But as they were preparing to stamp his passport, one of the Spanish guards told him in English, —*You realize this is the last time you can cross for a year?* —*What!* –he said, scooping up his passport just as the stamp was coming down. —*New restrictions by our government,* –the guard said. —*But I have a wife in the hospital.*—*Then you should stay.* –a senior officer said, stepping in front of the guard. –*But all our belongings are at our hotel in La Línea.* —*Leave your belongings behind,* –said the officer, —*or take her to a Spanish hospital. Spain does not recognize British claims on Gibraltar. You cannot play both sides against the middle.* He looked at the officer and the guard and the others there. No easy way around this, he decided.—*You have a telephone?* –he asked, thinking fast. —*Por favor…, Could you call my hotel and ask them to bring all our things to the border, and I'll pay them for it all when they get here?* The officials eyed each other, and then eyed him with a certain respect. —*Como no.* –said the officer, and he motioned for the guard to take up the phone.

Waiting for the things, he stepped outside the office and paced around. The guard came out and offered him a cigarette. They puffed away in silence, spewing their smoke into the cool air. Then the guard went inside to watch the "fútbol" game that was just getting underway. It was the same old story, century on century, he thought, envisioning the water and world beyond Gibraltar's great rock. But still, he could not duck the atavistic irony and had to articulate it with all the viciousness he was coming to relish: —*Caught in a fucking international mess over a woman's bleeding privates.* –he said to himself, spitting with bitter pleasure at the border dirt.

5.

He found the cheapest clean hotel he could and took a room next to a cockney-sounding couple from Australia. The next three days he measured out between trips to the hospital and excursions up and down the town's main street. The operation was successful, Dr. Johnson said, and she should be out within a couple of days. He brought her books and magazines, brought her postcards to send to her friends, tried to make small talk with her. But he was only allowed to stay an hour each day and spent the rest of his time dawdling in the shops and learning to despise each Indian merchant he chanced to meet. Now cut off from Spain, the rainy spell come to an end, the cup games over and a victor (he knew not who) established, he spent his hours, haggling with the merchants, savoring all the assorted foods of the town's restaurants and, on a high tide of horny fantasy, masturbating several times a day. In the evenings, he went to the movies and prowled around in a kind of sexual euphoria, never taking any step toward finding hooker or house, but just vaguely hoping he would happen upon at least one adventure before she came out of the hospital. But his luck was bad, his searches too timid. No adventures, no temptations, just the most banal of greetings from the Australian couple, not even an offer to share their bed, not even a flirtatious glance from a waitress, or even a faked come-on by a barmaid at one of the pubs by the docks. Just before she was due to leave the hospital, he visited a tourist office and worked out his exit plans.

6.

The doctor said she might bleed in the days to come, and that she needed rest and calm. She described her as physically and emotionally drained. At first she stayed at the hotel, watching the city's paltry action from the balcony, conversing trivially with the Australian couple. Then as she got stronger, they walked through the street together, making their way into the teeming merchant stores and the restaurants. One night they went to a movie and he reached over to take her hand, then went for her breasts, and later on started tonguing her ear. At each stage he felt a resistance which then abated. At midpoint in the film, she withdrew, crouching in the far corner of her chair. He looked over at her as she stared at the film, lost to him. He wanted to be in her mind, see how she saw all that had happened this month. Was he wrong in his perceptions? Was there another way to see it all? Was it something completely beyond him? —*You okay?* –was all he could muster to make conversation. —*Still bleeding.* –she said, staring at the film.

7.

He didn't want to know anything about the Indians or Australians did not want to particularize, humanize or empathize with any one around him. All his energies were intent on seeing how far they could now go on a journey back to each other. He knew that love was not the issue. He was the keeper of her organs and orgasms. Others were before him, others were perhaps simultaneous with him, still others, who knew how many others, might be when they were no longer together. Each day was a test, an opportunity, a catastrophe, a possibility.

So he approached her again a few days later, as they walked by the port, holding her hand in silence, turning her toward him. They walked back to the hotel and went to their room. Lying in bed, he began to manipulate her nipples, tonguing her, fondling and caressing, trying to kindle everything. Then, as in the theater, she pulled away. But he grew insistent, urgent, stroking her again, trying to win her ever so gradually back into his rhythm of things.

But how overcome all that had happened? The sense of blood and wound and hurt? Removing her lower garments, he began to stroke her clitoris with his fingers, as he kissed her firmly yet softly, and did the things she had trained him to do on these occasions. Slowly, tentatively, she began to enter into their old contract; everything began to coast and glide. But then the smell of her juices and blood came to his nostrils, and he was filled with a terrible desire to go down on her, to drink at her well, to suck out all the accumulated fluids, take them all in, take the hurt and wound and blood on to himself. Gradually, so gradually, he pressed his head down, where it had never been, where he now had to go.

—*No!* –she jerked away violently. —*No way, not on your life are you going to do that to me. That's something I might do, but no one does to me, not you, not any man, not any one, not even you know what I could die for.* He looked at her and took her in fully, understanding all too well the woman he'd chosen.

8.

Later that night, he sat alone on the terrace watching the little town go to sleep. No more rain, no *futbol.* Even the Christmas players and *falangistas* were no more. —*Bloody right!* –he said to himself, savoring the silly pun as he gave a sidewise glance in the direction of the Australians' room. And he wondered how it could be—a dumbshow whose depths he could not grasp: his life tied up with organs he would never kiss, all his energies for this being who probably wouldn't even be part of his life in a few years. —*What a fucking waste!* –he thought —*What a waste of energy and passion and disgust!* He tried to write something about it, but as always on this trip, he felt blocked, unable to write, when writing had been one of the reasons for his travels in the first place. But it wasn't all her fault, he knew it; he'd chosen his own poison.

9.

In the morning he showed her the brochure for the trip he had reserved on an Italian liner coming from New York en route to Mallorca and Sicily. It would be crazy to go back to Spain, he insisted, just a waste repeating routes they had traveled, sights they had seen. Better to go on, he urged, and she could rest on a cruise, really recover. And what's more the price was right, and all the details could be arranged in no time. —*I've heard this logic before.* –she grumbled, glared, but agreed finally. And off he went to the tourist office as if to buy the tickets he had in fact already purchased.

She, whose parents had come over from Calabria and Abruzzi by ship to New York, would now return to Italy, sailing through the Mediterranean with her U.S. *paisanos* eating huge plates of Alitalia Line pasta on the way to the land of their fathers. And he, wandering Jew who never even thought of visiting the places of his roots in Romania and Russia, would go with this woman who any day might no longer be part of his life, to Sicily, to Italy, to town after town, each day and each place an opportunity, a possibility, a catastrophe...

10.

Just about at this time, another Italian-American helped set off one of the first refusals that would mark a new generation whose ways would dominate the next few years to come. Living out old patterns to the limit in Europe didn't necessarily put you in tune with where you and others might be when you got back home. They had reached a limit, setting themselves on a rack of time that could hurt ever so much, but could not quite stretch them from who and where they were to the new time about to be born. The gates to Gibraltar would soon be closed. Conflicts over another waterway would change all. Soon they would be marching past the Duomo, singing *Bandera rosa,* shouting *"Americani imperialista!"*—the songs and slogans proclaiming a new era. Young quasi-Sartreans and beats, monadic nomads with Hemingwayesque hangovers, $5-A-Day guidebooks and a lust to consume "culture" at budget rates, they would fade into the background, replaced by self-styled dissidents and rebels, seeking a return to mystified roots or unrealizable utopias, eager to make their own ephemeral mark on time.

That afternoon, the Australians he'd refused to know checked out of the hotel, and the local radio station blared out heated debate over Franco's latest attack on

Gibraltar's status. As if in answer, some one announced a public reading of Neruda's civil war poems in the latest English translation. But they would not be there to hear of the blood in the streets. Two incompetents abroad, brought and bound together by the fragmented madness of their hopes and their ignorance, they ate at the hotel restaurant and then went to their room, to stare emptily at each other and ready their suitcases for the pathetic trip and the all too sad misadventures that would begin at dawn.

THE LITTLE BOY WHO FLEW AWAY

1.

Long before Christmas, David had stopped believing in Santa Claus. So long before that special day, alone in the house, he set out to find his presents, opening doors and closets and cupboards, opening boxes and bags wherever he found them. At last, under father's bed, he discovered a cluster of packages wrapped in green and held with red ribbon and scotch tape. Carefully he undid the tape and drew out the gifts inside. Then, after seeing all there was to see, he slid the gifts back in as neatly as he could, retaped the wrapping and returned the boxes to their place thinking no one would ever know.

So he was not surprised by the presents he found awaiting him on Christmas morning: the toys and games, the shirts and pants, the socks and ties. Only one gift did surprise him, one he had not seen or foreseen. He had given out the presents his parents had given him to give them and they had left to prepare for the people who would come to their restaurant for Christmas dinner, and it was only then that his sister handed him a small package.

"Here," she said, "I thought you should have one gift you didn't know about." He took the present, but kept his eyes on her face. "I know what you did," she said. "You think I don't know about you just because they're not here and they don't, but I do. I know all about you. ...Well, don't just stare at me. Open it. You got so many presents, you might as well get one more. ...Don't tear it open. Take it easy for once. I can save the paper. Look how grabby you are. Look how you tear things up."

It was a book: *The Little Boy Who Flew Away.* "Read what I wrote inside," said Fran. He opened the book and read the words written out in large red letters: *To David from his big sister, who knows he will understand.* On the title page was a picture of a young boy so fat that even squeezing and squeezing, he could not wedge his body through a wide doorway.

"Thank you," he said under his breath. "It's the story of a boy who liked eating more than anything," she said. "He ate and ate and got fatter and fatter. His parents told him not to eat, but he wouldn't stop. And one day he was so fat, he looked like a big balloon. ... See? Like in the picture. ... You can hardly see his arms and legs, or his head any more ... And ..." She flipped the pages to the back of the book where the fat boy was rising off the ground, while the others, the thin children, tried to hold him down. "'And a strong wind came along and blew him—up and away! Every one tried to stop him, but they couldn't. The wind kept blowing and blowing, lifting him up. ...'" She turned the page and showed him where the children and then the old people of the town looked up, straining their limbs, climbing ladders and trees. But no one could reach him. The little fat boy had become just a speck in the sky. "'Look at him go. See him go,' said the people. "My goodness ... he's gone.' He flew away and never came back," she read to him.

"I'm not that fat," said David. "You will be if you don't stop eating," she said. "You eat too much. You're always in the ice box. If I don't stop you, who will?" "I've tried to diet—all this month. I've skipped breakfast. I don't eat all the food you pack for lunch." "And what happens at dinner?" "I—" "I leave you dinner and when I come home, there's no cake or fruit or ice cream in the whole house. Sometimes there's no bread left. ... I can't even make a sandwich for you to take to school." "It isn't my fault you go out so much. You should stay home with me more. Mother says so. Then I wouldn't eat so much. You could stop me then." "I can't stay with you all the time. I have meetings at high school. I like to go to dances." He hung his head. "Oh, I know how it is. You don't like eating alone. There's no one forcing you not to either. You just eat to pass the time. First you take a little piece of pie, so little I won't notice. Then you take another, and then you think, maybe you better finish it all so maybe I won't remember. And then, before I get back, mother comes home and gives you something to eat. And sometimes even daddy comes home and you eat with him." "I like to eat with him." "I know, David. But you better watch out. Someday you'll eat so much, no one will sit near you. You'll get as fat as he is. You'll fly away." "That's not a true story, it's silly." "If you don't go on a diet, it'll be true all right." "You don't fly away if you get fatter, you stay on the ground." "Not if you're like a balloon, then you just fly away."

He went to his room and sat down at the desk staring out the window, not seeing anything outside. *She says she knows it all,* he thought. *But what does she know? She'll never know. I won't let her or any one know.* Now looking out the window, craning his neck, he could make out a portion of the street. It was snowing and no one was there. All the children all over the world were laughing with their families, playing with their toys. But his parents were working, and his sister was getting ready to go ice-skating with some friends. He opened a desk drawer and began to cram the little book inside. *I won't read it,* he said. *I won't.* Then he heard the wind rattle the window and watched the snow swirl and swirl. He turned the pages of the book. *It's getting worse,* he whispered, fanning the pages back and forth. *No. It shouldn't. No. But it is. It's getting worse. No!*

2.

It seemed to start that day in early December with the giggles of the boys in gym class. Mr. Wolfson was holding elimination races, and David and Melvin were the last two left. Both boys got down on all fours, Wolfson blew the whistle and they charged across the gym. As he ran panting along, he heard the laughing rise in his ears. "Look at them! Look!" cried the boys. Already tired, he ran as fast as he could. His legs dragged, he puffed and perspired. But he beat Melvin across the line.

The boys tittered and laughed and cheered, "Hooray!" "Yessir!" cried Mr. Wolfson. "They may not be the fastest, but they sure are the fattest," he said, bobbing his head and exchanging warm glances with the boys as they laughed and laughed.

Melvin laughed too. But not David. So all the laughter fell on him. "He's fatter than you are, David," said his friend Marty, keeping his face straight. "You're real—you're real plump, but he's the fattest one I ever saw." "Yeah, but he can take it," said Johnny. "Melvin can laugh, but look at David!" And the laughter broke out again. "Men! Men!" Mr. Wolfson admonished. "That's enough. The boys ran a good race. If they keep at it, they'll lose all that baby fat."

But they forgot the good race and remembered the fat. They remembered David's fat legs and his puffing. And they remembered his angry eyes. How those eyes had set them off! His winning told against him. Melvin sank into the background, but not David. In class Johnny put tacks on his chair and passed notes saying, "David is fat." Walking home across the school park, David and Marty were followed by Johnny's gang. "Fatso! Fatso!" "Leave him alone," said Marty. "Why do you stick up for him, Marty? You're not fat," said Johnny. "Just leave him alone." "Fatso! Fatso!" cried the boys. "Stop it!" David shouted. "Stop being fat," said Billie. "I'm not fat." "No," said Johnny, "you're skinny. You're the skinniest kid in school. You know why you're so smart in class? You're fat. You've got a fat head." "Don't listen to them," Marty advised. "Don't pay any attention and they'll get tired and leave you alone."

But he could not close his ears. He tried sometimes, even for days. "Look at him," the boys jeered, "he's getting so fat he can't even talk." He sucked in his breath and held it. "He's blowing up—blowing up!" they shouted. "Like a dead fish," said Billie. He clenched his teeth and fists but still said nothing. "Yeah, maybe he's dead," said Johnny. "Poke him, Billie. Go on." "Hey fatso," said Billie. "Hey Piggy," he said, poking David. "Stop it," said Marty. "Maybe he's got his mouth stuffed—with foo-ood!" said Johnny, pinching David's cheeks. So David opened his mouth and shouted, "Stop that! Stop it!" "Look," cried Billie, "what a fat mouth." "Fatso!" they all cried, coming at him, poking at him. "Fatso! Piggy!" "No!" he cried. "David is fat! David is fat! David is fat!" they chanted.

So it was no use. Each day the boys followed them. He and Marty tried to find new ways home, but the gang always found them out. Soon the December snows came, filling the school park and the street that ran along it to the big intersection at Town Street. and six, then eight, then ten boys lingered away from home and joined with Johnny. Then came Lois, one of the many new students who each day began arriving at the school after Thanksgiving break, and the first girl to join with Johnny. "David is fat!" cried Lois. "David is fat! David is fat!" they all cried, ranting and jeering all the way through the park to the Town Street crossing. Here the chants stopped short as the children came upon Officer Brown, who shuffled them off on their separate ways.

"It's just the leaders," Marty said one day. "If we could stop Johnny, the others would stop. I'll talk to him. He has nothing against me."

The last day before Christmas break Johnny tripped David in the hall. David scrambled to his feet and raised his fist, but Marty pushed him aside. "Johnny, why don't you leave him alone? He doesn't bother you." "I don't like fatsos," Johnny said. "And I don't like kids that can't take it." "Why can't you find some one else to pick on? You've been after him long enough." "Why can't you find some one else to walk home with?" "He lives next door to me. He's my friend." "Maybe you better make new friends. Why don't you walk home with me?" "You don't live near me." "You shouldn't walk home with him. We don't like it. Let him walk with Melvin." "He doesn't like Melvin" "But you like him," Johnny snarled. "Tell your fat friend to lose weight and then we'll stop. Even Mr. Wolfson says he's fat. Every one says so, maybe you should say so too."

School let out early in the afternoon for the holidays. David and Marty hurried into the park with Linda, another new student, who had just started at the school that day. "My mother said I should show her the way home," Marty explained. "Maybe she should go alone," David said. "I can't do that," said Linda. "That's not nice." "I've got to get her home," Marty said. "My mother said so." Linda kept lingering behind, stopping, dawdling, looking here and there about the park. "I've never seen so much snow. Look at it fall." "Come on," said David grimly. "You better hurry, Linda," Marty said, taking her hand and dragging her along. "Marty, I can't keep up. You're squeezing my hand!" "See anything?" Marty asked. The wind sprayed snow in his eyes. "I can't see them," he said. "See who?" asked Linda. "Why are we running, Marty? It's cold and mushy. Why don't we walk in the street like the other kids?" "If we get to Town Street, we'll be all right," Marty said, puffing. David tried to see the intersection. But they had wandered into a curving chain of high drifts. They couldn't see beyond the walls of snow. The wind whined and murmured. Town Street was far, far away, and they were already tired.

"I can't run any more," said Linda. "Maybe we can beat them," he said. "If we can get over the snow, we—" Suddenly he heard something whiz past his head. He glared at Marty. "Why are we running?" asked Linda. "Don't stop now," Marty pleaded, pulling her forward. "Marty—please!" "Is it them?" asked David. The wind now seemed mixed with a low murmur of laughter, which grew louder and louder. "What is it?" Linda asked. "What's wrong?" A snowball hit him on the left side. He turned toward the left and was hit on his right and in the face. "Ow!" cried Linda. "They beat us for sure," said Marty. "They're in front too." "Ow!" cried Linda. Snowballs came from all sides. "Ow!" she cried again. "Duck down!" Marty shouted, and the three clung close to the snow.

First arms, then capped heads appeared over the snowheaps. The air filled with snowballs. "Why are they throwing them? Who are they?" "Don't get scared, Linda. Don't get mad," David said. Voices rang out: "Merry Christmas, Santa Claus! Fatso! Fatso!" Linda stared suddenly at David. "Don't get mad," he said. "Ah-h!" she shrieked, hit again. She began to cry.

David made a snowball and cocked his arm. "David! Don't do it!" shouted Marty. "They'll only throw more. ...David!" But the snowball went flying. "Fatso can't take it!

Fatso can't take it!" The snowballs came faster. One hit Marty in the face. He reached down and made a snowball of his own. "Fat and Skinny! Mutt and Jeff!" "Look out, Marty!" warned David. But they hit Marty again and again. "Why are they hitting us?" Linda whimpered. "We didn't hurt them. It isn't fair." "I'm sorry," David said. He grasped the snow in his frozen hands. He threw wildly again and again. He had no time to pack them, they split in mid air.

"It won't work," said Marty. "We'll have to run past them." "We'll get hurt," said Linda. "If we get to the street, we can run to Town Street," said David. "They'll hurt us." "What else can we do, Linda?" said Marty. He took her by the hand and ran toward the street that ran along the park and led to the intersection.

David stood straight up and glared at the snow piles. "I hate you!" he cried. The voices echoed, "Ya! Ya! Fatso! Ya! Ya!" And more snowballs went crashing his way. He shielded his face, sidestepped, but was hit again and again. "I hate you all!" "Hurry up, David!" Marty called, and David scampered after him.

They could not see the street for the snow piles. But they made their way, followed by the snowballs and the jeering, chanting voices. "They're coming after us," David panted, seeing heads bob over the snow ridge and shadows against the white. "It's deeper where they are," Marty said. The snowballs came harder. "They're getting closer," Linda said. "It isn't fair," she cried, "it isn't fair." "Fat and Skinny," the voices chanted. "Mutt and Jeff!" "Stanley, Ollie!" "I can't see the street," Linda said. "I can't see anything." "Quick ... over the hill," Marty said, pulling her up the high icy pilings. "It's slippery." "Just a little more."

As they reached the top, the snowballs hit again. Linda and Marty bounded out of sight. David took a last look down on the field. "Look out, Fatso!" they called. "We can't miss you." They pelted him again, moving closer, closer. "Run, Fatso! Let's see Fatso run!" He gasped and wheezed in helpless rage as they hit him over and over. Then he started running, scrambling over the hill and skidding down the other side.

"They're coming after us!" he called up ahead. "Come on! Hurry!" Marty yelled. "You're so slow, David. Look! Come on! There's the corner! There's the policeman!" He ran after them down the slushy street, hearing his feet splash and his chest pant and heave. "Fatso! Look at Fatso go!" they called. Icy snowballs flew past him, splashing in slush, splattering against the street. "We'll get you again," one voice cried, "we'll get you every day after Christmas!" And one last wet and cold snowball landed on the back of his neck.

Linda and Marty slowed to a walk. He came up to them as they neared the corner, where Officer Brown waited to lead them across the street. "Hi kids," said the policeman, "A little late today, huh? Don't think I don't know what you've been up to," he said, smiling and winking at them as they reached the far corner. "You kids!" he said.

They walked on in silence, breathing hard, unwilling to speak or look at each other, kicking the slush before them. "They kept saying Merry Christmas," Linda said finally. "They don't know what Christmas is. ... They hit us because you're fat, didn't they? Didn't they say that?" "I'm sorry, Linda. I said you should go alone." "And Marty," she continued. "Why did they call you skinny? You're not that skinny. ... Marty! What's wrong? Why don't you look at us? ... Marty, your nose is bleeding!" "I got it from the first hit. When they called me skinny." "Does it hurt?" she asked. "It's real sore. I'll have to lie about it at home." "Why? Why don't you tell them what happened? David, why can't you tell your parents?"

He reached down and made a snowball. He smashed it against a tree trunk. "What're you going to do? They'll chase you again. They'll beat you up." Marty made a snowball and threw it against the same tree. "I'm sorry," David repeated angrily. "I know," said Marty. He put his hand to his nose again. "Maybe you better lose some weight. Maybe they won't pick on you then." He walked faster, dragging Linda with him. David kept pace, he stared down at the dirty slush. "It'll be alright after Christmas. ... We have ten days off. Maybe they'll forget about it." "Maybe," Marty muttered. "Maybe you better lose weight." "You know what?" said Linda, as they reached David's house. "I don't think you're fat, David. I didn't even think about it before they said it. You're just plump, David. That's all there is to it." David took her hand and squeezed it lightly. He half-smiled. "Maybe things will change," he said.

3.

On the night of Christmas Day, mother and father came home early. Mother slipped on an apron and started setting the table. Fran helped, while he and father watched.

"Only ten o'clock," said Fran. "Must've been a rough one." "We were short help," said mother. "But we sure did the business," said father. "Lines of people waiting—what lines!" "He gave them too much, he overstocked again," said mother. "Look at all this food, Fran. And there's plenty where this came from, believe me."

"Your father always orders too much." "You can never tell what's going to happen," said father. "They expect a little more on a holiday, and what if you don't have it?" He sat down at the table and popped a sweet pepper in his mouth. "No sir, you can't let them down at Christmas." "All I know is we work day and night, and for what?" "David, how are you son?" said father. "What did you do today?" "Marty went away with his family." "Played with your new toys, no? Sure were plenty. ... We had to work today, son, Christmas is one hell of a day—" "Marty—" "Since your father opened his dream house, we don't live like other people."

David winced. Mother always found ways to hurt. *Her face is always long, she's always tired, always complaining or yelling.* He wanted to know why. What was wrong? What was wrong with him and father?

Father put down his magazine and opened a bag. "I almost forgot, David. I brought home some extra goodies for you." And he handed some small cartons to mother.

Father was a stranger who lived in the house, who left before David got up and came back when he was asleep. But he was always happy to see father, until mother or Fran ruined it. They always did.

"Extra food again? That's all he needs." "Just a little treat, Fran." "You always bring home treats and he always eats them." Mother slammed a platter of turkey sandwiches on the table. "That's the least we can do is see he has enough to eat," she said, glaring at father. "Good food too, huh David?" Father winked at him, squeezing his shoulder. "Enough to eat!" squealed Fran. "You don't know what happens here. Don't you see how fat he's getting? Why don't you send him to bed?" "Since when do you take such an interest in your brother? You're always running off at the drop of a hat." "Don't pick on me because you're too busy to be with him." "Don't pick on him," mother returned. "I suppose I should never leave the house. Is that what you want?" "All right, stop it," said father. "Right now things are a little tight..." "His pants are tight." "Fran!" screeched mother. "Your mother and I have to work, and you'll have to make the best of it." "You're spoiling him, you do too much for him." "Why shouldn't we?" said father. "Why shouldn't we do all we can? ... You like it when we bring you good things to eat, don't you, son? You wouldn't want us to stop, would you?" He tried to eat his sandwich, but couldn't get it down. But father was having no trouble. Between bites, he smiled at David, and David tried to smile back. The two women turned hard angry eyes on father. *They hate him*, he thought. *Why do they hate him? How can he be so calm when they— ? What's wrong with him? What's he done?*

"Look mother," said Fran. "Look how much Daddy's eating. That's why David eats so much." "Don't you think you've had enough?" asked mother. "Just having a snack, eh son?" "Oh it's easy for you to make jokes. It's easy for you to smile and eat your fill. Trying to be the big man just because your friends got big. Working our lives away in the restaurant just to look big. And you are big all right..." "Like a blimp!" "Fran!" father said softly. "Want to end up like daddy?" his sister said. "Fran, please." "You'll fly away," she whispered in his ear.

"Well, it's true, he's putting on weight, just like you," said mother. "How many times did you eat today? How many times? Tell me!" "I have to sample the food, don't I?" father said. "I've had enough of your jokes," said mother. "We've heard them all: the big funny restaurant man, as big in size like his friends are in money. ... You've put on so much weight you're disgusting to be with." "Oh come on." "You can tell jokes, that's your business. It's yours, but you've dragged all of us into it. I have to keep after him all the time, Fran. Throwing away money just to look big, and each day we're getting poorer and poorer. I have to follow him around just to keep him in line." "Please," said father. "I'm tired of following, that's all. Look, look at me, see how old I'm getting. And look at him—so pink and happy."

For the first time he saw the deep lines on her face, the wrinkles around her eyes, the droop of her mouth at rest. "Please," said father. "Not in front of the boy." "You're the big man, aren't you? You're so thoughtful. They don't see you the way I do. You wear me out and I then I have to cope with them. I don't like my children to see me like this, but what can I do about it? I'm the one who has to yell at them. Haven't we punished them enough?" She began sobbing. "Just so you can be the big man." "Mother, don't cry, mother," said Fran crying with her. "You're no help, Fran. You don't do your share."

He began crying too, still not understanding fully. Father was the stranger, who was kind and full of jokes, always good, always kind and calm whenever he saw him, no matter how things were. But now he just sat there, and David began to understand the secret. Father looked so helpless, brooding across the table, looking at the others with dull, tired eyes floating in a sea of flesh. *He's calm because there's nothing he can do. He's fat.* And then he realized that father was not calm at all. Beneath his paunch were a pain and rage so terrible, he didn't dare let it out—the pain and rage of those who are fat. *Yes, he is fat,* David thought. *I've known it all along. He has that restaurant, he works, he stays away. That's why he's fat and that's why they hate him.*

They sat in silence, playing with their food, none of them really eating. Father patted his arm, but he squirmed away. "Well, this is one beautiful Christmas," said father. Mother raised her head and pushed the hair away from her eyes. "I guess we'll have to make the best of it after all." "Tell him about the surprise," father said eagerly. David looked from face to face. "Well, what happens next week, David?" asked mother. "The day before school starts..." "It's your birthday, stupid," said Fran. Don't tell me you can't remember. He must have things on his mind, he's in a daze." "You'll be—" father began, and then stopped. "He'll be nine," said mother. "You're going to have a party, son. We've invited all your classmates—" "All...my..." "Not all," said mother. "It's a small party." "Just before school," said Fran. "All right, not all," said father. "Just the important ones." "Just show him the list," said mother.

Father drew out his wallet and took a slip of paper from it, handing the slip to David. First on the list were Marty and Linda, then Lois, Billie, Johnny... "You don't look very excited," said mother. "He will be," said father, "when he sees the presents ... and the games we've planned...We're supplying all the food from the restaurant, David. You'll have the biggest, the best—" "You never had a party before," he said. "This year is different," said mother. "You always said it was too soon after Christmas." "It's true," said Fran. "He shouldn't have a party right after Christmas. The parents won't feel like buying extra presents. They'll think we're greedy." "Nonsense," said father. "They can give him some of their extra Christmas gifts."

He looked at his mother and father, then back at the list. "What's wrong, David?" Father extended his hand. "David—son!" "You didn't even ask him if he wanted all those kids," said Fran. "We wanted to surprise him," father said. "And now you've told him." "I won't be there. I wanted to see the look on his face." "Well, look. ... Maybe he doesn't like those kids." "My son gets along with every one." "Sure he does," said Fran. "He's so spoiled and demanding, every body loves him. He doesn't even play with Marty any more." "Why—why did you invite Johnny?" he asked. "What? — Oh, ask your mother, son. It's her list." "Johnny's mother's a new friend of ours, David. Don't you like Johnny?" "I—I...don't want a party." "You what?" said mother. "They'll laugh at me." "Don't be silly, David," she said sharply. "You're having a party. Every one's invited already." "Take it easy," said father. "Well I never heard such a thing. We try to make it up to the boy—" "You try too hard, mother," said Fran. "It only makes it worse." "It's the *way* you do it," said father. "The way I do it! This was your idea. You get all the ideas and I have to carry them out. I have to suffer for them."

"All right," said father. "So we don't have a party. Is that what you want, David?" For a moment he brightened. "I—" "Your mother will just have to call all the children and tell them we can't have a party after all. ... Of course, they might think it's funny. Maybe they've bought their presents..." He looked down at his plate, at his half-eaten sandwich. "The children may make fun of you, but so what? You know what's best for yourself. And if you don't want a party, that's all right by us. Your mother's almost in tears, she's so disappointed. But I guess we shouldn't try so hard for you. I guess we should let you go your own way." "All right ... all right," he muttered. "See how grateful he is," said Fran. "I knew you'd understand, son. Maybe I should've asked you before, but I wanted to surprise you. We can't turn around and tell every one not to come, can we? That wouldn't be right..." "No..." "Besides, you'll have a swell time, you'll see. You'll have the best fixings ever: sandwiches, cake. I'll have our baker—" "All right!" he cried. "All right!" And without looking back, he ran to his room.

4.

The night before his birthday, he dreamed that a large ball of snow rolled across the windy field getting bigger and bigger. Linda and Marty ran from it, swiftly rolling a ball of their own. Only theirs was black.

"Hello!" he called, trying to raise his voice above the wind. Linda waved her hand, but Marty kept pushing the ball. "Come on, Linda!" Marty called. "But Marty," she answered. "Marty!" he shouted. Marty pushed the ball aside, took Linda by the hand and stalked off the field. Linda waved frantically as Marty dragged her away. *He will be tall*, he thought as the wind died. *He'll smoke a pipe just like his father.* "Mmm," a man's voice said. "Mmm," said Marty's voice. Marty and his father, dressed the same, sat in identical chairs smoking identical pipes. David, dressed like an orchestra leader, snapped the stem of a pipe in two. "Bravo!" thousands cheered, clapping their hands. David bowed and Linda begged: "Marry me." "I'll consider it," he said. "Please!" she pleaded, kneeling before him. "Please! Please!" "Rise, Linda," he said with compassion. "I will marry you since you asked me. You are not perfect. But I will teach you in time." Water lapped against the ship, wind filled the mast, as they sailed away, she so pretty in her flowing gown, her head upon his shoulder as he steered toward the setting sun. But then when she drew back and smiled, it was not David who, with proud, loving eyes, turned from the helm to her. "Marty!" she cried with joy.

The wind howled. "It's coming! It's coming!" he shouted in panic. The black ball rolled toward him—faster, getting bigger, getting faster, bigger—huge ... crashing against the bowling pins!

And now his stomach grew and grew—and grew a mouth that talked to him. "Mmm, that was good," said the stomach in a voice that was high-pitched and wheedling, cheerful, yet insistent, all at once. "Mmm, yes, I want more." Thousands of children watched him and laughed as he sat on a stage surrounded by heaps of food, stacks and stacks of meats and pies and cakes. Helplessly he stuffed himself, as the laughter rose and his stomach demanded: "Yes more. Mmm...more. Give me more. I won't ever stop." "No," said David, stuffing his mouth. "Eat I say. You wouldn't want to make me die. If I die, you die. So eat. Fill me up. Make me grow."

Trucks roared along the highways blowing their horns; airplanes zoomed by in formation; trains from all points made their way to the stage where he sat. "Eat, eat," said his stomach over and over again. "More," it said, "more," while the children and now adults—all the people of the world—clapped their hands in rhythm and chanted, "Look at him go, see him go!" By truck, by plane, by train the food poured in. Begging hands, brown, black, yellow and white, reached out, but the food went into the stacks and heaps beyond the hungry and angry people. The stacks of food grew, and so did his stomach. "My goodness," said the people. "My goodness, he's gone," they said, their voices fading away. "Please," he whispered, "Please."

And then the stomach, the people disappeared. Father and mother hovered over him as he continued to eat. "Grr," growled mother. "Grr," growled father. They growled at each other in hatred, then smiled sweetly down on him. "Our boy," they simpered. Mother's tired face grew older and older. Father grew younger, slimmer. His eyes slanted up, his hair turned red. And on his head, he sprouted two horns. "You wouldn't want us to stop, would you, David? Ha! Ha! Ha!"

And now father's laughter merged with the laughter of the boys and girls, with their rhythmic handclapping and their chanting. "David is fat, David is fat," they chanted. They formed a circle in his living room, laughing, chanting and clapping their hands, linking their arms, Linda and Marty now with them, and other, new boys and girls with strangely twisted and blurred faces moving around in a circle that ever grew tighter and smaller. The floor was covered with shattered dishes and toys. The party table was overturned. Sandwiches lay in red pools of punch. And amid the wreckage he sat, crying wildly, licking punch-stained icing off huge pieces of birthday cake. The children sang, laughing louder and circling around him, but it was not the usual song:

> Happy birthday,
> Happy happy birthday,
> This is your day,
> But we have all the fun.

Their singing and laughter rose to a roar, as they spun faster and faster around him. And in the din, familiar voices blurted out, spurring the laughter on. "You kids," said Officer Brown. "You'll fly away," said Fran. "Men, men!" said Mr. Wolfson. "Mmm," said Marty's father. "Mmm," said Marty. "Grr," said mother. "Grr," said father. "If I die, you die," said the stomach.

"No, no...No!" he shouted, sitting up in bed. "It's not my party. It's a little boy's—someplace else. I'm not invited." But the party was his—and he knew it. "All right...all right. It's going to happen. Well, let it...let it!" And, moved by the force of dreams, he knew what he had to do.

5.

They gathered in the living room, sitting primly in their seats, looking shy, guilty almost. They followed his movements, afraid to speak, waiting. Finally, smiling at him, Marty broke the silence. "Did you have a nice Christmas, Billie?" "We went to the parade. What did you do, David?" "I stayed home by myself." "That's no way to have Christmas," said Lois. "His parents work," said Marty. "Did you have enough to eat?" Johnny asked. The children stifled their giggles.

Mother returned from the hall, where she had placed the coats and presents. "Children, don't just sit there. Why are you sitting around?" "Johnny doesn't like the party," he said. "David," Linda warned. "That's not true, is it Johnny?" "Well...there's nothing to do," he dared. "But you just got here." "My mother says this party's silly," said Lois. "It's right after Christmas." Mother wiped her forehead with the edge of her apron. "We thought David should have a party," she said. "It's not his fault his birthday's today...David, why didn't you show them the game your father bought. You know... Pin the tail—" "Yeah," said Johnny, "we play that all the time." "Not with a prize like this," said mother, taking a package off the table. It was wrapped in green paper and with a red ribbon. She shook it seductively. "What is it?" asked Lois. "Don't worry, you'll see. Now you children play while I get the refreshments ready. You've never seen such a spread—" Johnny began to laugh. "What's so funny?" mother asked. "Let's play," said David. "David, stop looking so mopey," she said. "He's so mopey these days, you'd think he didn't want a party. And here I stayed home from work. And his father went to all—" "Let's play!" he said. "Let's eat!" said Billie. "Yes...yes... in a little while, she said, retreating to the kitchen.

"She's funny," said Lois. "She's so fidgety." "That's cause she works," said Billie. "My mother doesn't work, does yours?" "No," said Lois. "She says that's not nice." "That's why I'm so funny," David said. The children stared. "Let's play," said Linda. "All right, Linda," he said. "Here's the blindfold. Girls first."

Linda, then Lois, then Marty took their turns. They were spun around and then set free. They tripped and bumped into furniture. At last they found the donkey on the wall, stabbing him in the eye, in the leg. Marty hit the white space. Then Johnny took his turn and pinned the tail low on the donkey's rump. "You win, Johnny," said Lois. "That was real good," said Linda. "I haven't gone yet," said Billie. "Neither have I," said David. "Hey! Gimme that blindfold," Billie said. "That's not fair, David," said Linda. "You should go last." "It's my party." "That's why it's not fair." "What's fair's fair," said Marty. "Linda's right." He glared at them, and then fastened the blindfold. "All right," said Marty. "All right."

He spun himself round and round. Johnny grabbed his arm and spun him faster, pushing him toward the wall away from the donkey. He groped along the wall, trying to find the sheet of paper. "You're getting warm," said Johnny. But he reached out his hand and touched the door trim. "You're lying," he said. He made his way to the adjacent wall, carefully skirting a chair. "That's not fair," said Billie. "He knows the room." "That's all right, Billie. Let him go," said Marty. *The table is next,* he told himself. He raised his hand higher to avoid knocking pictures and knick-knacks off the tier table. "Johnny," said Marty. But it was too late. Johnny jarred him against the table, and some objects crashed to the floor. The children scrambled around the table. "Look at that!" said Johnny. "Look at the mess he's made." "Look!" said Billie. "Let me see," said Lois. "Ooh is he fat!" "And look at David," said Johnny, and they laughed. He hurried along the wall, turned the corner, and reached out for the donkey. "Don't, Billie," said Linda. As he jabbed the pin into the donkey, Billie slammed against his knees, and he toppled to the floor. "Look," said Johnny. "Just like his old man." He came over to David and jabbed him. "Stop it!" David cried. "Like father like son," Billie snarled, just above a whisper.

He ripped off the blindfold and stared into the leering faces of Johnny and Billie. He turned his head and saw Marty whispering in Linda's ear. Linda saw him first and nudged Marty. They frowned at him guiltily. In Linda's hand was the picture of father. "Johnny won," said Lois. "You pinned the tail on the belly." "You did not win," he said. "Why not, fatso?" said Johnny, elbowing him. "Quit poking!" "You're fat like your old man," said Billie. "Don't call him—" "You're so fat, you couldn't win," said Johnny. "I did win." "David..." said Linda, her voice trailing off. "See, Linda?" said Marty. "You shouldn't even try to win at your own party," said Lois. "He's fat," said Johnny. "He wants everything. That's why he has a party so soon." "That's right," he answered. "I want all I can get. It's my birthday and I should win." "Look at the prize," said Billie. "An old Christmas present, and he wants that too." "That's not so." "You're a hog. You're—" "Children!" mother said.

She ran into the room, wiping her hands on her apron. They turned to her as she looked at the pictures scattered on the floor. "Johnny won," said Lois. "Johnny won and David says he won. He didn't win, he knocked over the pictures." "David, shame on you," said mother. "You shouldn't even try to win." "I don't care." "Here, David," she said, handing him the prize. "Give it to Johnny." "I—" "Give it to Johnny." He held his breath and handed over the package. "Thank you," said Johnny. "Now let's have no more of this," said mother. "Let's go into the kitchen and have something to eat. David, pick up the pictures."

Giggling and whispering, they followed mother into the kitchen. Linda and Marty stopped at the door and looked back at him, but he turned away. When they were gone, he stooped down and lifted the picture of father. There he was, standing in front of a banquet spread, surrounded by the cooking crew, a fat man with his arm on the shoulder of his fat son. A diagonal crack in the glass sliced the picture in half. "Ooh!" they exclaimed in the kitchen. "David's father made this. We own a restaurant," mother said. *It's happening*, he thought. *It's happening and I don't care.* "David!" mother called. He placed the picture on the table, facedown. And, drawing a deep breath, he marched into the kitchen.

"Don't stuff yourselves," said mother, as they devoured the food she served. "Save room for the cake." Wearing glossy New Year's party hats, they sat around the table, eating from platters filled with cocktail sandwiches of tuna, salami, cream cheese and jelly, drinking from cups brimming with red punch. "There's so much here, we'll never eat it all," said Lois. "Just do your best. David's father didn't want you to go away hungry. David, why don't you put on your hat?" "I don't want to." "Don't be that way. The other children..." "No." "Stop stuffing yourself, David. What are you trying to do?" "Eat," he mumbled, his mouth fully stuffed. "Eat as much as I can." They began to laugh. "It isn't funny," said mother. "You eat too much as it is." "He's too fat, isn't he?" asked Johnny. "David! Pick up your hat! ... I don't understand, you're acting awful!" He answered by gobbling another sandwich. "Stop eating, David. Pick up your hat this instant." "He's a bad kid," said Billie. "Just like Johnny says." "He certainly is," said mother. "And if he doesn't stop he'll have his father to deal with. David, if you don't stop, I'll send the children home."

But he wouldn't stop. He reached both hands across the table, snaring bits of food at random, reaching again as soon as the food was packed in his mouth. "Send them home," he said. "Then I'll have more to eat." "I've never seen you this way, David." "Maybe you better bring the cake," said Linda. "Then he'll have to stop." "Yes, Linda. That's a good idea." She crossed to the pantry, opened the door, and, her hand resting on the door knob, she looked back. "I don't understand. I've never seen him like this." And she left the room.

"See how sad you made her, David?" said Linda. "That's no way to act. After she's gone to all this trouble—" He plucked a sandwich from her plate and swallowed it. "David!" "Why don't you tell me I'm bad, Marty? That's what you want to do, and now you can." "You see, Marty," said Johnny. "You are bad. You're right," Marty said at last. "Ooh!" Lois cried. Mother stood before the pantry door, holding a huge white cake with nine candles on it. "Happy birthday," they sang.

"How do you like that for a cake?" said mother proudly. "I never saw one so big," said Lois. "Just right for me," he said. "I'll eat it all." "No you won't," said mother. "You'll have no more than any one else, I'll see to that. Every one will take some cake home with them." "No they won't," he said. "Now listen here, David. Every one will get the same amount. I'm going to cut this cake, and when I do, I don't want to hear another word, not one word. You don't deserve all this as it is. I've overlooked a lot, because it's your birthday, but there's a limit to what I can take."

"What's that sticking out of the cake?" asked Billie. "It looks like a penny," said Lois. "That's right," said mother. "This is a special cake—a money cake. David's father had it filled with coins, with nickels, dimes, quarters, pennies. There's even a half a dollar for the lucky one." "Ooh, money's dirty," said Linda. "No, Linda, they're boiled in water, they're all clean as a whistle." "Whistles are dirty," said Johnny. Billie laughed, “Only fat ones.” “We keep all the money?” asked Lois. “Of course you do.” “I’ll get the most,” said David. “We’ll see about that,” said mother. “You get what you get.” “I want the silver dollar,” he said. “It’s a half dollar, hog,” said Billie. “In one minute, you’ll get absolutely nothing, understand?” “Light the candles.” Mother struck a match and lit the candles one by one. “There,” she said. “Now, make a wish, David, and blow them out.” He stood up and closed his eyes. And with all his might he made his wish. *I wish I get the biggest piece with the most money, he wished. I wish they get almost nothing. And that they beg me for a penny.* Then he leaned over the cake and blew as hard as he could. “You got them all,” said mother. “Now take a knife and make the first cut... From the middle—that’s it. Now let me take over.” “I want the biggest piece,” he said. “For once in your life, you’ll get the same as every one else,” she said, carefully cutting even slices. “Here, Linda, Johnny...”

“That’s not big enough,” he said when he received his share. “It’s not as big as Billie’s.” “That’s all you’re getting,” said mother. “I have a dime and a quarter,” said Johnny. “Three pennies and a nickel,” said Billie. “Children, don’t chop up your cake, it won’t taste good.” “Who has the half dollar?” he asked. “Marty, do you—?” Marty nodded and held up a shiny half dollar. “Gee, Marty, you’re lucky,” said Linda. “It’s not right,” he said. “I only got a nickel.” “Now, David, stop pouting,” said mother. “Eat your cake like every one else.” He reached across the table and grabbed another piece. “David!” she screamed and slapped him. “There. I told you you couldn’t have ay more. You’ve asked for that all afternoon.” “I don’t care,” he said. “On your birthday,” she said. “Give me the cake. Why should Marty have the most?” “He’s real bad,” said Billie. “He’s spoiled.” “I want the cake. I should have the most.” “Well, you’re not getting any more,” said mother. “I’ve coddled you enough.” “You hate me, that’s why. You gave more on purpose. And they hate me. You all hate me.” “David, I’m warning you for the last time. If you carry on, I’ll send the children home—and their presents with them.” “Let them have their presents, see if I care.”

He lunged at the cake and threw it on the floor. “David!” Linda cried. “He’s bad,” said Johnny. “He should be spanked,” said Billie. “That’s all,” mother said, her voice full of anger. “That’s all I can bear.” “Send them home,” he said. “I hate you, I hate all of you.” “I’ve got two quarters,” Johnny whispered to him. He pushed his hands against the table, lifting it with all his might, as he leaned back on his chair and toppled to the floor. The cups of punch fell over; the punch bowl slid off the table and crashed to the floor. The children jumped from their seats. “Send them home,” he said sobbing wildly. “Then I’ll eat everything.” “Look at him,” said Lois, astonished.

"All right, children. I'm sorry," said mother. "Pick up your coins." "David's bad, isn't he?" asked Marty. "He's worse than that, Marty," said mother. "Don't worry, it's not your fault... All of you, come on. Out of the kitchen."

They moved to the other room, their voices getting further and further away. "You'll have to go home," he heard mother say. "Here, let me give you back your presents." "Do we have to do that?" "I'm sorry, Linda, he's got to learn." He heard them move into the front parlor, heard mother helping them on with their coats. For an instant, he thought of calling, begging them to come back. But then, he felt a kind of darkness fill him, he could not speak nor think nor hear at all. Finally, mother's footsteps sounded louder and louder, until she entered the kitchen. She tried to put away some dishes, but then sat down, sighing and breathing deeply. The only sounds were their breathing and punch drip-dropping off the table. "David, David," she sobbed. "I'm sorry—" "Don't you tell me you're sorry. How could you do a thing like this after all we did?" "I—" "They'll go home to their parents and tell them. They'll say I don't know how to raise you." "You don't care about me," he said, all his bitterness returning. "Not care about you... Just let your father hear that when he gets home. Just let him hear what his wonderful son did today." "Tell him," he said. "Let him beat me with his strap." "All right," she said. "That's just what he'll do." "Let him," he said with terror and pleasure. "Let him!"

6.

He managed to get through the first day of school, and when the final bell rang, he broke from the lines of children and hurried into School Street. The wind whistled, and only after walking for some time did he realize that Linda and Marty were just a few steps behind him. "Well?" he said, stopping and glaring at them. "Don't do it, Marty," he heard Linda say. "Come on," Marty answered, "I've got to." "You don't want him to walk with me, do you, Linda?" "It isn't that, David, he—" "I thought I should tell you, David," said Marty. "I can't walk home with you any more." "I knew you'd say that." "It's not what you think," Marty said. "My mother told me not to walk home with you. She didn't like me getting hurt." "That's a lie," he said. "No it's not." "I told him not to listen to her, David. But he can't. She's his mother." "Why are you walking with me now? I didn't ask you to." "I wanted to tell you," said Marty. "I don't want to walk with you. I want to walk by myself." He started walking again. Marty and Linda followed him. "David, you *make* the kids hurt you," said Linda. "It's none of your business what I do. You're not my friend." "But David—" "There he is!" a voice cried out. He looked around and saw Johnny and Billie and other children running toward him. "Don't look at me," said Marty. "I didn't know." "What are we going to do?" Linda asked. He put his hands on his hips, took a deep breath, and moved a few paces toward the children.

"You can't run away this time," said Billie, coming up to him. "No, I can't run like you," he answered. "I'm too fat to run. Besides, I don't have to run." "You're fat all right," said Johnny. "Fat like your old man." "I'm not fat like him. I'm fat like no one else." "My mother says your restaurant's no good," said Lois. "So what?" "That's why you're fat," she said. "She says only a real bad boy would do what you did." "So what?" "Can't you leave him alone?" said Linda. "I thought you and your girl weren't going to walk with him, Skinny," said Johnny. "He's not walking with me. He's on your side and so's she. You're all skinny," he said. "I'm better than you." "You're fat," said Billie. "You're a bad kid." "Fatsos are better. They're stronger." "Oh yeah?" said Billie. "Hey Shannon, you hear that?" "Oh yeah," said a tall boy with a sneering face, coming up to the children with a group of his own. "Who's this, Billie?" "My cousin Shannon's who. And all his friends," said Billie. "He's in the fifth grade. I told him what you did."

"You think fat kids are stronger, fatso?" said Shannon. "Don't answer him, David," said Linda. "He's too big." "They—they live longer," he said. "Skinny people don't eat enough...You'll all die before me. And Marty first." "David!" Linda cried. "It's true," he howled bitterly. "Fat kids are stronger. I can beat you all up." "Don't let him say that, Shan," said a scrawny friend of Shannon. "Show these little kids." David backed toward the snow drifts on the curb. "I'm not afraid of you," he said. "You're a fake. You're all fakes." "Hit "im, Shannon," the children cried. "Hit "im in the belly." "I'll show you...I'll show you I'm not afraid," said David. "You think so," said Shannon, cocking his arm and moving toward him.

He shoved David against the snow drift. Top snow fell on David's head, and they laughed. He wiped the snow from his eyes and moved to the other side of a trash can across from Shannon. A large crowd of children gathered now. He saw them laughing and biting their lower lips with excitement. He began stalking Shannon around the trash can, cocking his fist. Shannon backed away, with mock fear.

"You still think you're stronger, Fatso? You think you can beat me up?" "Look at him, Shannon," said Billie. "He's shaking. He's chicken. He's a fat chicken. He won't fight." "Hit "im anyway," said Shannon's scrawny friend. "Hit "im in the belly."

"Naw," said Shannon, mocking. "You think I really should?" "Don't fight, David," said Linda. "They'll all know now." "Fatso! Fatso! Chicken!" shouted the children. "Hey!" Shannon cried.

David sprang at him and knocked him over the trash can. He grabbed his arms and yanked him into the snow drift. "Come on, Shannon! Hit him! Get him!" Shannon tried to push David off, but the snow gave and he sank deeper into the drift. "He's too heavy for "im! He can't get up!" Lois cried. David let off some pressure and Shannon pushed him away, standing up. "Now I'll show you," Shannon said, panting. But David rushed him and they both fell down. Over and over they rolled, but David landed on top and pressed Shannon's arms into the slushy street. "Get up! Get up, Shannon!" the children cried. Shannon twisted and turned but he couldn't get up. "Give up," said David. "Say I'm stronger." "Get off me!" Shannon squealed. "Not till you say I'm stronger. Say it!" He held his breath, waiting for some word, some sign from the others.

"Let him up, fatso," said Billie. "Not till he says I'm stronger." "You're not stronger, you're fatter," said Johnny. But the only sign was a snowball that thumped against his back. And now they pelted him with snowballs. They scooped up the spilt garbage and hurled oranges and bananas, empty milk cartons. He began crying, smashing Shannon's hands against the icy asphalt again and again. "Ow! Ow!" cried Shannon. "Help me!" "Give up," David chanted madly. "Give up! Give up!" "Look out, David!" Linda cried. Shannon's friend rushed forward and clutched at David's arms. Marty ran over and tried to pull the friend off. "Let him go!" said Marty. "He won." Shannon's friend pulled David off and squared for a fight. But David pushed him away and clutched at Marty. "Look out Marty!" called Linda. "I don't need you!" said David, wrestling Marty to the ground. "I don't need your help." "I know," said Marty. "Ow! I know!" "Here comes the cop!" said Billie.

Officer Brown pushed the children left and right. "Okay, you kids. Break it up. ... You, David, get up. ... David!" He loosed his hold and stood up. Marty rolled over and scrambled to his feet. "David started it," said Johnny. "I saw it all," said Officer Brown. "I've had my eyes open for some time. I'm surprised, David, real surprised. You fighting—and with Marty. You're turning bad is what you are." "You should see what he did yesterday," said Lois. "I can guess," said Officer Brown. "Now you—David!"

He broke from the children and climbed up on the high snow pile, out of the grasp of Officer Brown. "David, I'm gonna report this," warned Officer Brown as the wind began to rise. "I don't care what you do," he answered. "Now you get down from there. You get down." But he climbed higher and higher, and entered the snow-filled park. "David!" Linda cried mournfully, her voice now far away. "They'll all know now—the whole school...every one!" "Want to come with me?" he dared her. "I can't, David," she called. "I have to go with Marty. My mother—" "Then I'm glad," he said. "Let the whole school know. Tell my folks. Tell every one. I'm better than all of you." "Come back, David!" Officer Brown called. The wind whined and whistled, the children raised their arms toward him. "Fatso! Fatso!" they called, their voices rising above the wind.

He looked down at them, clustered around the policemen, in silhouette against the snow. There was Marty and Linda and Lois and Officer Brown himself, and Johnny and Billie and Shannon and all Shannon's friends. And others—a multitude of others—others all together, arm in arm, all against him, forever. "I'm stronger and fatter," he called. "And I'll stay fat. Even if I get thin, I'll still be fat. I won't change for any of you!" The wind rose, and again they raised their arms and waved. Their lips moved, forming words of derision. But they were tiny now, and their voices were faint and far away.

Valentine's Day, 1947

1.

The door reflects dull hall light. He turns key and knob, then draws back hands, flexing them, thrusting the cold out along his fingers - the outside cold, away. From a pocket he takes the crumpled letter:

To Susan

He breaks the seal, tugs to free the card, cracking a bond of paste. Thick red-paper heart-lopsided, ragged: deep pencil-scars crisscross around the edge —here, there; in the center, dry bubbles of paste seep out through holes in a white paper doily, and below, in black on the red:

Love David

He yanks the light cord. In the dark his breath comes short and loud. He yanks again. The cord trembles, the string weight ticks from wall to wall. Cramming heart and envelope into his pocket, he opens the door and steps inside. Pivoting, he kicks some last snow flakes at the floor mat, slams the door and calls:

"Ee-laine! Are you home? Ee-laine!"

2.

Under the window, dirty unscraped dishes and pots crowd the drainboard and peer over the rim of the sinkwell. Below, on the floor, a box brimming with garbage, a column of ants invading, parading on the brown table, amid the bread and cake crumbs, the spilt sugar.

The clock is yellow, a blur almost. Outside the window, it is grey flecked with white… *It's late.* He undoes his coat, flings it on a chair, then stands perfectly still. Faucet drips carom off water-filled plates, the clock whirrs… No other sound… except a low murmur from the stove. Vapor rises from two black pots. On the stove-tray, a red and white tin can—a tin-can, big-hatted chef smiles and holds out a platter of spaghetti… *She is home.*

He takes up his coat and hangs it on the hook, rushes out of the kitchen and down the dark, narrow corridor, past all the rooms and doors, into the living-room and then, turning off to the side, into her room: cold and cluttered, and loud with the grind and moan of cars and cars plodding through slush. "Come on, Ee-laine! Where are you?" *She's stepped out for a minute –or…* He swishes through the dresses and sweaters in the closet, crouches and squints under chairs, under the bed, past the shoes and dust - even under father's desk. "Come on, Ee –" He rises, his body rigid, tensed: *She's not fooling this time, she's dead! -or run far away—away… This dark house forever - with no one!…* Saying softly: "Elaine?"

He runs back along the corridor. "Elaine ... please!" He stops… A crackle —loud, *too loud: the turning of a page? … Yes—of course*! Under the bathroom door, a seam of light. "Here you are Elaine. I found you." Another page turned, thundered. *Her games*! "You can't fool me, Elaine. You're in the bathroom. You're reading a magazine" Silence… a page. "Elaine, it's me-David!" *Not a game? ...No one home after all.... Or - maybe it's not her, but some murderer, some kidnapper.* "Please, Elaine, talk to me- please!" Another page. "You are here! It's you!" Silence. "It isn't fair… Why don't you talk to me? If you don't talk to me, I'll do something you won't like." Silence. He shakes the door knob. Not a sound. "I'm warning you, Elaine. You better talk to me." He rattles the knob - louder, louder. "Elaine! The house is on fire! Ooh, it's terrible! Big red flames, Elaine! Big red flames.... Ooh - oh! They're coming closer! Ooh! I'm burning! Elaine! Save me! I'm burning - burning!" The flames leap up, scorch his skin, singe his hair.

Before him, the bathroom door; in his hand, the door knob - free. He bounces it, then smashes it back into place — his voice shaking, pained: "Come on, Elaine, talk to me. Please talk to me!" Bracing up against the far wall, crashing into the door again, again. "You're not fair. I'll tell mother - that's what I'll do." He sobs wildly, spiraling down to the floor, his hands twisting the knob. "Why don't you talk to me? Why?"

A sharp tear of paper. He catches his sob and drops his arms, letting the knob click back. A plunge of water, a rustle of clothes, her shoes scuffle across the tiles. His fingers probe cracks in the dry, worn linoleum.

She is inches away now. He tenses his neck, rushes fists to his temples. The latch is turned, the door squeals open. His chin pressed against his chest, his knees against his stomach. He does not hear her footsteps and barely feels her skirt brush against him. Yet somehow knowing she has passed, he turns to see her… not walking, but almost marching - stiffly, evenly, not too fast - toward the kitchen, entering it, closing, and not even slamming, the kitchen door behind her.

Not even slamming the door! His eyes shut, his lips curve up. His face is taut crockery: it trembles, shatters and crumbles. He tries to stop the crying, muffles — the sound only. Tears streak his face, sting his cheeks. He tries to wipe them away, but fails. The tears bring tears. *Let her cook dinner. Let her! I won't eat it. I'll never eat her food again. I won't. Never.*

He takes slow, deep breaths. Crying and breathing become one rhythm… slower… slower… Now there is silence, no sound from the kitchen… *She will not come to see me.* He stabs her with a long knife, stabs again and again; she lies on the floor — in blood! … It's too quiet. There is no clink of silver, no water running on metal... Silence.... *But what is she doing?*

He clenches his fists and, his back against the wall, edges toward the door. Paper rustles faintly, a chair rocks, creaks. *Is she crying? She doesn't cry. Why should I?* Who can tell what she does? She has cruel secrets, she frowns quietly, her moods, shift like bats. *Why doesn't she smile?* She can be so nice - prettier than any one ... *than Susan*? He reaches into his pocket, past the letter, touching finally the cold piece of metal, taking it out. Heart-shaped locket of gold, reflecting the light overhead—a pale wavering moon. He draws in the chain his hand swallows the locket and closes. "Prettier than Susan," he whispers.

He thrusts the locket back. His eyes close slowly, then blink open. *Prettier than mother*? His hand moving back and forth along the chipped plaster of the wall. *You should love mother more —daddy too. I never see them. They have to work — they have to make money now.* Fingers digging into the wall: *They always stay away....* Again he looks toward the door, trying to see through it. So kind sometimes: She gave him her music notebooks and helped him paste in pictures of composers, and now they were choosing ones for a new book on singers (he cried when she said they couldn't keep the one of the tall black man dressed as a general or emperor because he didn't love his country — he'd tried to hide it, but she had found it). She keeps the books locked up in her bottom dresser drawer, it is their secret.... Dropping his hand, pushing the door open, crying: "I'm sorry, Elaine." He runs into the kitchen.

3.

She dabs her cheeks with pink tissue, her elbows on the table. She does not look up, and he approaches slower. "Elaine, I didn't mean anything ... I'm sorry." She turns to the wall, crushing the tissue in her hand. "Go away," she says. "But I didn't mean it. I — I thought you were dead." It is not even her —just a blouse, hands and arms, long black hair over shoulders. "Elaine! I didn't mean it!"

"You didn't mean it!" she screams. "I told you never to speak to me when I'm in the bathroom." "But I thought you were dead. I didn't hear you." "You're lying. I've always got to take care of you, and all you do is talk and talk: Elaine this, Elaine that." She turns to him, her eyes glaring, forcing him back. "I'm sixteen years old — sixteen. And I never have a moment to myself."

An ant scurries between his shoes, cut off from its clan, lost. "I have to take care of you all the time. Listen to you, cook for you, stay home with you — even on weekends. I haven't gone out in three weeks." "We went to the movies." "Danny and I took you with us." "Elaine, I'm sorry. I'll tell you what: you can go out tonight ~ I'll stay by myself." "And who'll take care of you?" "I don't need anyone." "You're afraid of the dark." "I am not — I'll leave on the lights." "Sure — sure! And what happens when the kidnappers come?" His trembling fingers drum on his lips. "No— it's not your fault.... Besides, where would I go? Now – *now*! ...'

"You've already messed up tonight - and everything. It just isn't fair. You get everything you want: "You're such a little boy!" But I -I don't even have a room to myself or a mirror - She stops, her head lolls on her shoulder.

"What's wrong, Elaine?" "Nothing - leave me alone." "Can't I do anything? Tell me what's wrong." She looks up, her eyes glinting. "I have to spend all my time with you and you won't leave me alone. Aren't I entitled to anything?" "I'm sorry, Elaine. I'll be good. I won't bother you any more." "I can't even have any dates. I always have to take you or have boys over. And you're always in the way: "I'm sorry." "It isn't right for me to always have boys over." I'm -" "If you say you're sorry once more, I'll kill you, you spoiled brat. I'll take a knife and cut off your head." He closes his eyes and covers his ears. "I'll cut off your head and then I won't have to see you or hear you any more. And I'll have some peace and quiet."

4.

Before him, a plate of spaghetti. "Tuck your napkin in, I said. You'll get it all over you.... That's it." His fork trembles, catches the light overhead. "What's wrong? Can't you be still?" *Roll it on your fork, it slips off; get it to your mouth, it trails along your chin, leaves a smear of greasy red.* "Don't play with your food, eat it: His teeth chatter, he cannot stop them. He twirls the spaghetti round and round. "Come on, eat it: She shouldn't talk with her mouth full. The spaghetti drips on his chin, slides back onto the plate. He covers his mouth.

'Oh, you're such a baby: She leans over him, snatching his fork. "Look at yourself. You've got sauce all over your face… And now you're crying just because you've got sauce on your face: "I am not crying. I won't ever cry again: "I'll bet. Men don't cry, but you'll always cry, you're crying right now: He turns to the wall, she chops away at his spaghetti: *ka-plank, ka-plank.* "I don't know what's to become of you. David. You're so sensitive about everything.... Look, David. I've got sauce on me too: Slowly he turns. "You do not: "Here, look close: Her lipstick-red lips - around them, a fringe of dull orange-red.

'Well?" Suddenly she sticks out her tongue, licks the tip of his nose. "Ha! Ha! Isn't that funny?... And look-on my blouse too." Tiny polkadots of orange-red on the white sticking out. "Yes, that's funny," he says, laughing with his sister. She cuts off her laugh, he jams his to a halt. She scowls. "What's wrong, Elaine?"

Scowls more, more. "Please –" a great bubble rises from her stomach and ... explodes in her mouth. She laughs and laughs, rocking back and forth, stamping her feet, shaking her head from side to side. "Oh David, you're such a fraidy cat." Pointing her finger at him: "you're so funny. Ha! Ha!" Her glowing black hair swishes this way and that; he smiles, nodding shyly, laughing again. "Now come on," she orders. "Before it gets cold."

She returns to her chair and begins to eat; then he begins. She laughs again, spaghetti spurting out of her mouth onto the table. He yanks his mouthful down:

"Look what you did, Elaine." She keeps chewing, bending from the waist, swaying, laughing with her mouth open.

And now he dares to ask his question: "Did you get my valentine?" Again his plate, the rhythmic eating. "Yes. But you shouldn't have done it. You wasted your money." He nibbles his food, says nothing. The spaghetti is paste, he plays with it. She keeps on: fork up, food in.

'Full already?" she says between bites. "I'm not hungry." He smiles weakly and drops his fork. "That's good. I made such a nice dessert and now I can eat it all by myself." She smacks her lips. "What is it?" "Oh, never mind. You're not hungry." She goes on eating, she hums a tune. "Come on, Elaine." "You really want to know?" "Yes - come on, tell me what it is." "No, you don't want dessert. You're too fat anyway." "I'm hungry. Elaine! I'm hungry!" "You're just saying that not to hurt my feelings because you know I spent a lot of time making that dessert." "No I'm not." "You don't care?" "I didn't mean that - please!" "Well I'm not sure..." "With sugar on it - come on!" "All right, but if you don't like it, you better keep quiet."

She stretches, yawns, and humming her tune, rises and walks slowly to the refrigerator, opening the door and standing in front of the shelves so he can't see. He bites his lip, waits. She glances over he shoulder. "Close your eyes." "Oh, Elaine." "Come on, close your eyes."

Silver splotches erupt in the dark. Her skirt rustles.... She approaches - her lips stretched down, fangs instead of teeth; close-pinched, inflamed eyes - wild grey-streaked hair. Her bony long-nailed fingers hold a knife. The huge blade catches the kitchen light, blinds him. She plunges the knife—!

"Stop shaking your legs, David. Do you have to go to the bathroom?... Stop peeking. Don't you have any patience?" He covers his eyes again, but he has seen.

"Happy Valentine's Day to you—'

A cake - chocolate and pink, heart-shaped, with *DAVID* in red jelly.

"Valentine's Day, dear David—'

He throws his arms around her neck, jumping up and down. "Thought I'd forgotten you.... Come on, David, sit down." "It looks so good." The fork slips from his hand, he picks it up. "You really shouldn't have cake, you're getting so fat." "But it's Valentine's Day, Elaine." She cranes her neck toward the clock, squinting. "Yes, Valentine's Day."

5.

He swallows the D, the A and the V. She takes the dishes from the table, stacks them on the drainboard. “Elaine?...” “Yes ...” “Well.... Can we listen to your records ... and ... work on the music notebooks? Can we?” She lifts some plates out of the sink, onto the drainboard – *slam!* “I can’t.” “Why not?” “I can’t. I have something to do.” “You never help me, Elaine. You always promise.” “And you always want things you shouldn’t want.”

She looks up at the clock, presses the plate edge against her chest and stares at him darkly. “You never help me,” he says weakly. “I can’t and that’s that.” “It’s not fair.” She peers toward the hall, drums her fingers on the plate. “I’m always alone,” he says. “Fair ... I’m the one who’s not fair!” “What, Elaine?” “You didn’t offer me any cake.” He bites his lip.”... You want some?” “I had to remind you first.” “I’m sorry. Elaine. Here.” “No, I don’t want it. If you’re so stingy you won’t give me one small piece.” “But here, Elaine.” “You just forgot that nice people share with each other. But you never felt like giving any cake to your sister.” “That’s not so.” *Why does she look at the clock*? ... Almost 7:30. “Liar!” She jams the plate into the rack. “You’re just a little liar who has to have his own way. Self self self. All the time.”

Once more he offers the cake. It rolls off— onto the table, bounding to the floor. “Look at the mess you’ve made. Look!” “I’m—” “Look at it. I swear! I don’t know what to do with you. All I give up - all the time. When I could be going out, I stay here with you. Cleaning your nose, wiping your behind.” On his hands and knees, he fumbles after crumbs. “Get up from there, David. Of all the stupid things to do. Go away. Go and wash yourself’

6.

The door locked, he washes his face of the heatsting, the redness; then sits, doubled over, elbows grooving his thighs, his hands cupped under his chin. The room is narrow and damp. His breathing fills it, reaches every corner, rings the iron pipes. His sounds echo, return evenly, the same— yet somehow magnified: freer, more final, complete. He is the room. Nothing can harm him. The mirror on the wall reflects the wall.

But suddenly, the scraping of plates, the distant clash of silver. *If I breathe louder...* But he cannot help swallowing air and leaning forward: the scuffle of shoes, the rising dirge of water turned on... then, a sharp ring —close by, off to the side; again— from *their room.* The water dies; footsteps tap nearer, pass by— hitting faster, then stopping. A half-ring. "Hello, Danny..."A door squeaks, clicks.

He reaches past the card, drawing out the locket. Not looking, he traces his finger around the edge, stopping at the chainloop, starting again. Helplessly, he tries to hear, caching: "Danny... Danny... But Danny -" She slams the receiver, the door hits the wall. She runs past him again, through the livingroom. *She's going to her room.*

Now his room shrinks, while he grows bigger - monstrous. His limbs press all four walls. He is cramped and squeezed, the ceiling bows his head. He cannot move or breathe, and yet — he grows.

On the ceiling, paint has peeled in all directions, plaster bare in the center.

"David!" He sits up as she draws closer, closer to the door. "David!" The knob turns. "David, open up. I've got to speak to you." "What do you want?" I've got to speak to you — please!" He goes to the door, stands before it: he clenches his hand around the locket, puts it behind his back. "David!" He hesitates and… opens the door.

"In my bottom dresser drawer, David.... You know, the locket Danny gave me ... you know the one... I've got to have it." He steps back. "I don't have it." "But it's not there. You're the only one who knew where it was— in the drawer under the notebooks ... I told you yesterday I had to give it back ... and it's not there!" "I don't have your locket." His face wells with heat, again he steps back. "David, I've got to have that locket. I won't punish you, I promise. If you know where it is, please give it to me ... please." She starts to cry. "I won't hurt you, David. But I've got to have it." Crying, her legs tottering. "You won't hurt me?" Her eyes meet him. "David — no! ...You have it?"

He shuts his eyes and holds out his hand. "In your hand!?" He opens his fist, palm up, not seeing her at all: the small locket— old, tarnished, reflecting the bathroom light: the pale, misshapen moon. "Thank you, David." "The chain's broken." "Broken?" "I broke it." "That's all right, David. I can tell Danny— " She stops. The floor, a checkerboard of tiles — black and white. "David, did you mean to give this to someone?" "I gave it." "Gave it!... But —'He springs for the door. She grabs him by the shoulders. "Let me go! Let me go!" He tries to wrench free. "Not till you tell me who you—" "I won't!" He lunges again. "Tell me." "I gave it to Susan for her birthday last week. I had to give her something... I thought you wouldn't care. I gave it to her." "But it was my locket." "I know, I know!" "Well...?" "Well, yesterday you said you had to give it back, and today I asked Susan for it, and she said, ask Mary Alt

—and I saw Mary Alt wearing it. I said where'd you get that, and she said Susan gave it to her. I said, give it to me. But she wouldn't.... So I ripped it off her neck. And she started crying. And—and Miss McCarthy sent me to the principal and I sat in her office all afternoon. And I missed the party." "David!" "I didn't think you'd care." "Poor David." "I didn't think."

Everything blurs. Her warm hands caress his neck. "Poor David." "Hit me if you want." He falls against her. That's right, David. You cry." He tries to break away. "I'm sorry, David. Don't worry. I'll leave you ... by yourself. When you're ready, you come in and help me. There's a mob of dishes to do." She kisses his forehead. "Just take your time."

7.

He does not walk at all, it is the floor that moves —moves not only across, but slowly, slowly up, lifting him into the kitchen— without his doing anything but stare at the floor, not yet awake, not knowing. But he has not collided with chairs or walk, and he is in the kitchen.

'Don't stand there like a corpse. Get a towel." He takes one down, doubling it over his arm, then lifting it and pinching along the fold. "Hurry. I've nowhere to put the dishes."

A large stack already — from yesterday, this morning, tonight: different-colored plates and pots and glasses in the draining rack, reflecting the dull light. "Don't look so down-hearted.... There aren't that many." Carefully, without upsetting the others, he removes a plate and begins wiping - slowly. Finishing, he places it on the table, takes up another, wipes it... wearily. He closes his eyes, and all the dishes — the whole ugly terrible heap: solid, cold — fly off the edge of the spinning globe. Calendar pages flip over and dishes sit in piles to be cleaned and hidden behind cabinet doors — dumbly, wearily ... again, again: endlessly. *Work ... yes! Work is what's so bad....* Again the dishes, the silverware fly away. Everything disappears from the face of the earth.

"Come on ... I put your cake in the icebox. You can have it later." He smiles weakly, affects a big, manly voice— drying a glass: "So many dishes, Elaine. So many dishes." She throws a towel over her head, grabs the broom and leans on it— puckering her lips and speaking in a high, squeaking voice: "So many dishes to wash. I don't know when I'll rest. So many dishes." "Oh, I don't look like that." "That's you." "No, it isn't." "So many dishes to wash." "You've got a towel on your head. You're not supposed to." "You've got me there." She takes off the towel, casts the broom aside. "Really, Elaine, it doesn't seem like we'll ever stop doing dishes." "That's right. It shall go on forever and ever. Your whole life shall be spent drying dishes ... if you don't start drying."

She turns on the water, sprays the pots and pans. Reluctantly, he takes up a plate, working now fast, now slow. He starts, stops" stares, starts again. He dries and redries the same dish.

"David..." She stares out the window, her back to him. "Yes, Elaine?" "Danny's coming over.... That's why I need to give him back the … the locket?" "He's taking someone else to the dance tonight... at school. And I said it's all over.... That's why I had to have the locket... to give it back." "Over?" "Yes," she says, turning to him - her face so pretty, so plump.... *Her eyes are so sad.* He raises his hand and gropes clumsily along her cheek. "It's all right David. It's not so bad, not so bad at all. And look: When Danny comes, I want you to say hello and shake his hand. And then I want you to say good night and go to your room. Understand?" "Yes." "Then let's finish these dishes."

She takes her towel and helps him dry. He barely moves "David, smile." "I hate it here, Elaine." "We won't be here always." "Someday you'll be married, won't you?" "I guess so, David… Maybe …I hope so." "And you'll go far away and live in the country. I won't see you." "You'll see me. Besides, that's a long time from now. You'll be a man then. It won't matter so much."

Outside the snow is still falling— white spots against tall shadowy buildings. He cranes his neck to see beyond them. "Elaine?... Not tonight, but some time ... when you get a chance - you know... Well, could you help me work on the notebook - of singers... Just to get me started.... We don't have to have one you don't want." "I'll help you tomorrow night. I promise." "You always promise." "Well, this time I mean it. Tomorrow night I'll help you." "Swear to God and cross your heart, no—" "No crossed fingers.... Now smile.... That's a little better." "If you can't make it tomorrow, Sunday's fine." "Tomorrow night... I promise."

She looks him up and down and exclaims, "David!"; she turns away, then back suddenly. "David ... I know what: Let's build a city." "What do you mean?" "Let's build New York - with dishes, silly." He creases his chin. "Here." She goes to the table and puts a glass in a saucer, dries a fork and sticks it in the glass, asking, "What's that?" "Give me a hint." "The saucers are an island."… "The —the Statue of Liberty!" They laugh. "You see? We can build a whole city while we dry the dishes. We'll try and guess what we build."

Quickly, he dries two cups, turns them upside down on the table, and lays a fork across. “What’s that?” “I don’t know.” “Oh yes you do. Come on.” “I know!” “Sure you do!” “It’s a telephone!”

“No!” “Why, sure it is. Here, look at the—” “Elaine, it’s not a telephone. It’s the George Washington Bridge.” “Oh ... oh!” “You knew what it was.” “No I didn’t. I thought—” “Come on, Elaine. Don’t lie. Come on. You knew it was the George Washington Bridge.” “No, I swear…” “Come on, Elaine.” He laughs suddenly. “You knew and you just said that. You just tried to fool me, didn’t you? Didn’t you?” They both bend with laughter. They laugh and laugh. Then she hands him a pot. She curtseys, he bows - and they set to work building their city, while the snow falls and the light seems to make the dishes glitter and dazzle.

THE LANDLORD

1.

At first Mr. Hirsh would come home from work carrying his paper, and if you were bending over, he'd swat you and say "hi, boy," and you'd look up and see a red face laughing and sad fuzzy eyes suddenly lit up.

We wondered why the lit up eyes seemed so sad, but we didn't say it out loud. We only knew that Mr. Hirsh was wonderful-to be always laughing when his eyes were so sad: that was something.

We didn't have much time for old people. We came home from school, had our milk and cookies, and then stood outside thumping the ball against the stoop, letting it bounce up and trying to catch it before it bounced again.

But Mr. Hirsh came into the game, and he didn't have to win all the time. He'd say, "I'm Joe DiMaggio who are you?" Bobby was Dixie Walker, and I was stuck with Sid Gordon. But it was all right. Sometimes Sid Gordon could win.

And Mr. Hirsh knew not to play too much. Instead, he trimmed the bushes along the walk, so the ball wouldn't get stuck. And when we'd lose one, he'd get another. With all these bushes, you're bound to lose a few," he'd say and it's my fault." But we knew it wasn't. Sometimes the ball would end in the sewer, but he'd pretend it was lost in the bushes and still get us another one—fast too. He said he'd come home from work and hunted them while we were at school. But we knew that wasn't so.

Of course we never told him we knew, we were so happy to keep on playing. And after a while we'd say the ball was lost in the bushes, even when they went down the sewer. We'd say that without his saying it first. And we knew we were lying, and

I even think he knew we knew. But he took it to mean we were friends I guess, and still got us new balls just as we thought he would. Then we really started lying, saying we'd lost balls when we hadn't. And what could Mr. Hirsh do? He was stuck with his story about the bushes. We got a lot of balls that way.

That was in the fall. My parents had just moved into the neighborhood. They worked long hours and weren't around much. Mr. and Mrs. Hirsh were the landlords. Bobby lived next door. He had lots of friends, but he played ball with me.

In the winter it wasn't stoopball because of the snow but it was Christmas and sledding. Mr. Hirsh bought me and Bobby a sled, and he'd go over to the park with us and watch us sometimes and join in too. Only there wasn't any way we could play games with him now or make the most of him. He didn't seem so old now. He almost seemed like one of us. We liked it better in the fall.

One day Bobby said, "Mr. Hirsh's got gray hair and wrinkles." That was a silly thing to say. Any fool could see it. But I saw Bobby had a special reason to talk. "My mother says his face is red "cause he's got a bad heart and the blood's all going to his head. She says he'll die before long." "Yeah?" I say, "Well, my mother said Mrs. Hirsh's pregnant," he says. "What's that?" "She's pregnant—that's what she said. And she said he's pretty old."

I couldn't get what Bobby meant. But soon I saw that Mrs. Hirsh was getting really fat in a funny way, and she and Mr. Hirsh looked happy. I could hear them laughing a lot upstairs. And they were always going out now, like never before, and having lots of people over, and there was so much laughing and yelling I couldn't sleep sometimes at night. And Mr. Hirsh didn't have that sad look any more. I knew what that was, I'd seen it all before. I said to Bobby, "Mrs. Hirsh isn't pregnant, she's gonna have a baby." And Bobby said, "That's what pregnant is." But I knew I was right and he was wrong. He was just trying to slide into being right. That's the way Bobby was. With him I was always Sid Gordon.

So I began to look at Mr. Hirsh in a special way now. We didn't like this baby because we knew what it would do to us. We were waiting for the spring because we wanted a big stash of pink balls. Bobby said we could have a raffle like at church and make money. But we had only ten balls between us, and you couldn't make much that way. We knew what happened when people had babies.

So we had to look at Mr. Hirsh in a different way now. Not that he changed much, but he did change some, you could see it. He still said hi and swatted us, and went to the park and brought us candy sometimes. But more often he'd stay home because his wife was sick, he'd say. And even when he'd go, he'd get a dreamy look and say something he'd said before— like "It's so cold your nose could break off," something silly like that. And he'd sound hollow, like the sound came through a straw stuck in his throat. You could tell he wasn't in the park but somewhere else— in Mrs. Hirsh's stomach, I guessed. He just wasn't with us.

"My mother says he's rehearsing," Bobby said. "What's that?" That Bobby always came up with words you couldn't understand— just so if he was wrong he could say he was right later. "Like in a play. She says he's rehearsing at being a father."

Well, that explained it. And all along we thought we'd had him charmed— the way you can do it with old people that are lonely and sad with troubles, and wish they were kids again. You can really take those kind. But here he'd been taking *us*. We were his baby till that baby came— and soon there wouldn't be any pink balls or anything.

Sure enough, some weeks went by and Mr. Hirsh stopped going to the park. He'd still be friendly, but he didn't care much about us. We could see it. We were mad, only what could we do? We talked it out one day walking home from school.

"We gotta do something," I said. "We sure do," Bobby said. But I could tell he just said that, he didn't care much. He'd only make some plans you could never use, and then when one of mine didn't work, he'd say I told you so. Nothing mattered that much to him. He could always go back to his friends or go home and have a good time. But he and Mr. Hirsh were the only ones I talked to.

So Bobby just did as usual, saying what I'd said, waiting for me to make a plan so he could say how silly it was and then make some crazy one you could never do. But that wasn't because it wasn't a good plan— oh no! It was the plan, only he'd have to work it with a Sid Gordon. That's the way he was.

I had to think of something but I couldn't. So I started talking, thinking maybe I'd get so worked up, I'd dream up something so good, Bobby'd have to go along. "You know what he's done. Now he's gonna have a kid and I bet he won't even let us play on that stoop. He won't even let us breathe too loud." "But what can we do?" said Bobby. He wanted to look like he meant business, to make me make a fool of myself. But this time I fooled *him*— because I was worked up and I'd already hit on a plan.

"We'll just not go with him to the park. And if he comes anyway or finds us out, we won't pay any attention to him. We'll act like he's not there." "That's no good," Bobby said, like always. "He's still fun sometimes, so why spoil things ahead of time?" "Because if he can't rehearse now, he won't be a good father. And then he won't have fun unless we're around." "It's no good." And now I knew Bobby was saying no for sure this time. "He's stopped rehearsing," he said.

I was so mad I could scream. And I just looked at him— with his red hair and pushed-up nose. He was Dixie Walker all right. And what got me mad was he just wanted to look smart. He wasn't thinking about that raffle either. He just didn't care that much. He just stood there trying to think up a crazy plan we couldn't do, so we'd end up doing nothing. And I knew I had to think up another too. I knew I had to out-Bobby Bobby. And the funny thing is, I did it— and fast too, before he said a thing. "Ok, Mr. Dixie Walker bigshot," I said, "I've got one you can't say no to."

Well that stopped him. I never came back with another one before, and he wasn't too happy about it. All he could say is, "Yeah? What is it?" "Stop the baby." "What?" "He wants a baby, right? So, stop the baby!" You could see he'd never heard anything so wild and didn't even believe I could think it up. So now he said, "Ok Sid Gordon, you tell me. How do you stop the baby?"

And then I said it all, my eyes flashing into the trees and along the snow piles — like I'd discovered gold. I said it all and changed everything — felt things I'd never felt before, and changed everything inside me, fast. "Easy," I said. "Mrs. Hirsh's got it. In her belly, right? ... And Mr. Hirsh is never home all day, is he? ... So one day when he's at work, we go up to Mrs. Hirsh and say, Mrs. Hirsh, someone's calling you downstairs. You better go see. And soon as she starts down, we come up behind her and give her a push, and down she goes— woosh! And then— and then—."

I was stuck, I couldn't finish. But not Bobby. He was jumping up and down, pushing off on my shoulder. "No more baby?" he shouts. Something hurt in my stomach. I didn't know what it was or why— not yet. But it started when I was talking and now I just watched Bobby and hurt more. "Stop the baby!" he was yelling. "We get a rope and tie it across the stairs, so when we push she'll go down for sure! We got a rope too— on the sled?"

"It's no good," I said, and I stopped in the street. "But you just said—" "I changed my mind. I know it won't work now. You can't stop babies." "But I saw it on TV. This man kills his kid—woosh! down the stairs!" "I won't do it. I can't." And all at once I was crying— like a fool. I turned my head so he wouldn't see.

"I don't get it," Bobby said. "You think up a good way to get at old Hirsh—" And now I was getting mad and I knew I couldn't hold it back for long. "I don't want to think," I said. "I don't want a plan." "Come on, David. It's a neat idea—" "I don't want your ideas. I had enough of them." "Mine!" "Just like yours." "Well, jeez, you don't have to — say!" He tried to spin me around. "Leave me alone!" I shouted.

"I get it," he said, getting sharp all at once. "You don't want to hurt old Hirsh." "No," I said. "I don't." "You don't want to woosh!— down the stairs!" "Stop it Bobby." He kept flying at me— "Woosh! Woosh!" "Stop it!" "You don't like it."

"That's right," I said. "I don't like it and I don't like you because you made me think it and you like it. I don't like your plans— or TV shows or raffles. And they don't mean a thing anyway."

And now Bobby was mad, because he thought I wasn't fair. And he was right in a way, I guess, but in another way he wasn't. "You like Mr. Hirsch," he said. And he started dancing and chanting around me. "You like Mr. Hirsh!" "Better than you any day." Bobby stopped. "Ok. You like him. When that baby comes, he won't even look at you." "That's not true. I won't let that happen!" "No! I won't. Me! "Cause I'll... stop the baby!" "No!"

"Woosh!" he shouted, dancing again. "If you won't, I will! I'll stop it! Woosh!" And then he hit me hard in the belly, and then he ran and said, "You wait." And I just sat down against a bank of snow all hurt and scared inside.

2.

So now everything was turned around. And I thought what a big fool I was, but there was nothing I could do about it now. I just thought, Bobby is gone and Mr. Hirsh is on his way. And I thought ok, if that's how it has to be, ok. I'll go after Mr. Hirsh and try not to lose him. Ill be such a friend of his, he won't forget me for anything.

And I had a way to be his friend, because what if Bobby really tried to stop the baby? And I felt good for a minute thinking I really had a job to do. And then I had that hurt feeling in my stomach again, and felt bad for all kinds of things, like for taking the pink balls. Then I got scared, because I could almost see what Bobby was planning. And I thought how stupid it all was and how Mr. Hirsh wouldn't be my friend no matter what, so I couldn't warn him because he might not believe me and ask questions and get mad— or something like that. But I said, if Bobby's going to stop the baby, you've got to stop him. And I felt better and decided to get to work and stop thinking, which was smart, because that's what started my trouble anyhow.

But I found out there wasn't too much I could do. The first few days I'd meet Mr. Hirsh coming home, but we just couldn't seem to talk to each other. He'd still bring presents, but not for me. And he didn't try to swat me or say let's go to the park. He didn't even ask why Bobby didn't play with me any more— why Bobby was back with his old gang and I was by myself. It was bad. Every day I'd just say some words that didn't mean a thing and then I'd try to hint at the real thing. But I couldn't get it out, especially when you could tell he just wanted to go upstairs. So after a while, I didn't try hard to see him anymore. He looked all nervous and worried anyway, and I decided I'd do better right now just keeping my eyes open.

But the less I saw Mr. Hirsh, the more worried I got, watching for Bobby, afraid he'd make his move. He didn't do a thing, but that just made me see he was trying to get my guard down. He even tried to talk to me once, but I wouldn't give him the chance to fool me. And after that, whenever I'd see him, he'd go woosh! and laugh at me. That's all he'd say—and those friends of his said it too: "Woosh!" they'd shout at me. The worst of it was, I'd see him all the time because I had to make sure he didn't try something, and seeing him made me remember all the good times we'd had. That didn't make me want to talk to him really. But I was getting lonely—more and more. I had no one to say a thing to, except my parents when they came home from work late at night. And they didn't say much. Some days, except for school, all I heard was *woosh!* I'd come home and have cookies and then turn on my dad's victrola. And all the time I'd be looking out the window, waiting for Bobby. And then Mr. Hirsh'd come home and wave hi and go upstairs, and I knew Mrs. Hirsh was safe another day. I wouldn't have to worry after that, but somehow it didn't help much. I felt empty in my stomach then. And it wasn't that I didn't like victrola music. I got to like it better all the time.

Day after day I just sat there listening and watching and every day I got more lonely and scared. And I wanted time to stop, but I knew it wouldn't. And I knew I should tell Mr. Hirsh, but then I'd think maybe it's not going to happen. Then I'd turn up a symphony loud to drown me out, and I'd try to see how Bobby'd do it. I'd drift away in the music and see someone wearing a mask tip-toe up the back stairs. You couldn't see his face, but it had to be Bobby. And each day he'd get a step higher and closer to Mrs. Hirsh. And she'd scream *David*! because I was the only one home I guess. And I'd run up and stop him just in time. And Mr. Hirsh would thank me and give me something good. And after that I'd feel good and then I felt empty again. So soon I kept it a secret and didn't let them know how I'd saved them. But it was getting harder all the time. Each day Bobby got higher and closer and I just did stop him. And now he carried a gun and now a knife. And the gun and the knife got bigger, and we were running out of steps.

Then in the schoolyard Bobby yelled, "Hey David! My mother says it's any day now." And, like a plan, I looked around and saw Penny Carter skipping rope and the rope went *woosh, woosh*! And I knew what it all meant. Mrs. Hirsh was having her baby soon and Bobby was going to get her first. Not with a gun or a knife. But with a rope just the way he said.

It was a race. All the way home, I saw Bobby in his mask climbing the stairs and me chasing after, and Mrs. Hirsh tripped over Penny Carter's rope and screamed. And then the scream was the baby's, and, Mr. Hirsh stood there holding the baby and smiling. And I don't know which made me feel worse. But I knew I couldn't stand it any more. I knew it was my last chance with Mr. Hirsh. I'd have to tell him now, even though I didn't want to and was scared of him and what he'd say. In some way I didn't want the waiting to end. I wanted it to go on forever if it only didn't hurt so much. I always knew I'd have to tell him and take my chances, and that really scared me and gave me that empty feeling more than anything.

After Mr. Hirsh came home, I heard him shoveling coal in the cellar furnace. I knew this was it. I took a deep breath and went downstairs. Sure enough he was there. But when I saw him, I froze. He was learning over his shovel and staring into the fire. His face was bright red from embers, and his eyes were bright too. His teeth showed all white, and I thought, if he laughs it's the end of the world. I just had to stay still and wait for him to get back to work and look like Mr. Hirsh. But he just stood there a long time and didn't move. I had to say something or we'd be there always. "Mr. Hirsh," I said. But I must have whispered it, because he still didn't move. Now I thought it wasn't him, so I shrieked, "Mr. Hirsh!" And this time he heard me and it was him. He moved out of the light and said hi. "Hi," I said. "Can I give you a hand?" "That's ok, David, just one more to go."

It was like I wasn't there. He went over to the bin and lifted a shovelful of coal. And I looked all around trying to find I don't know what. There were piles of soggy newspaper and rags all over. The outside was blocked by snow on the windows. Even with the heat it was cold and damp. There wasn't a thing I could do, and I wanted to go away. But I couldn't get my feet to take me—not now.

Mr. Hirsh poured coal on the fire and shut the door, then he walked over to his worktable. On it was an upside-down basket with rocking horse legs standing in the air. While he looked at it, I came down off the stairs and moved close up to him.

"It's for the baby," he said, rubbing his hand along the side. "I'm sanding it down." "Can I help?" "No thanks. Not enough work for two." He started folding a piece of sandpaper. "Mr. Hirsh, I hardly see you any more." "Oh I see you." But he was turned away from me, didn't even look up. "No, you always go right up to Mrs. Hirsh. You didn't even tell me about the baby."

He squinted at me hard, his eyes hard. "Your folks told you… " He didn't wait for an answer, he started scraping the wood. "I guess I should've done it," he said in a quiet voice. And then he got louder. "But you found out anyway… everyone did… They couldn't believe it—I couldn't… at first." He wasn't talking to me. He was soft and loud and now he was soft again and a little sad. "But it's true— any day now" "Mr. Hirsh!" He looked up, his lips were tight, and his face was bright red from the light by the table. "Yes." "… Nothing."

And now he looked down at the basket again, as if I hadn't said a thing. "It's my old cradle," he said. "Fifty-four years old… I got him lots of new things… You'd think maybe—" "It'll be fine, Mr. Hirsh." He was quiet for a minute, we just stood there. "What color you gonna paint her?" "Blue," he said. And now he sanded one of the rockers— a long time. I looked around the table and shelves at the jars of nails and screws— and then at a stack of dusty old magazines. I picked one up and looked through it. It looked all right, but then I couldn't read anymore, so I put it down. And then on the shelf I saw a bucket.

"This the paint?" "Uh huh-" he said, not looking up. "Can I see?" I jumped up to get it, and on the way down, I bumped against the cradle. It would have crashed, but Mr. Hirsh stopped it. He grabbed the bucket from me and pried the lid. "You see now?" he said, sticking it in my nose. Then he closed it and put it back— all before I could see it— and started sanding again. "Could I help you when you start painting?" And this time he breathed deep and looked me in the eye. "It's a small cradle— for a baby, see? It only takes minutes to paint— and I want to do it."

"Sorry," I said. I mean I heard it come out. And then I was so mad at saying it, I said, "You don't want me around, do you?" "Now, David—" "You used to play with me and Bobby. But now—" "David, it's just that Mrs. Hirsh needs me now— and there's so much to do."

But I knew he was just saying that, and besides, I had to start telling him. "You don't even know about Bobby. You don't even know we're not friends anymore." "You and Bobby—?" "You didn't even know." "I been so busy, David, I—" "You don't even know us anymore. When that baby comes—" "When my kid's here, we'll all be friends."

Well that stopped me and I couldn't say it. Because I knew then that the reason I was going to was so he'd say what he just said— and I knew that wasn't right. So I looked at him hard and said, "How can you be friends with a baby, Mr. Hirsh?"

"Not friends, but... " He couldn't finish it. I just turned away and picked up the magazine. After a while he said, "You and Bobby had a fight, huh? Well, kids always fight, you'll get over it." And that got me mad, so I tried again. "Bobby's gonna stop—" "I know, David, I know." But he didn't. He just didn't care. And all at once I missed Bobby and it didn't seem right to tell on him— not for Mr. Hirsh. If he didn't care, why should I? "Anyway," he said, "You've got other kids to play with."

"I don't have any kids!" I screamed. "They're all Bobby's friends anyway. They all stick with him. I don't have anyone!" And I said this to give him a last chance— to see what he would say. And I knew all over again I had to tell; no matter what he thought of me or Bobby or what I thought of him, or why I told, he had to know. But just then, Mr. Hirsh changed the subject.

"Look, David." He picked up the stack of magazines. "How'd you like to have them? They're full of pictures and stories— see? Like the one you're looking at. Lots of things about pirates and ships . . ." He kept turning pages and showing me all this stuff. And I did like pirates and pictures, but I couldn't look at them. Besides, Mr. Hirsh was blocking the light, but he would never think of that. "Like to have "em?" he said.

I felt so tired, all the blood was draining out of me. Those weeks of watching were too much trouble, and all Mr. Hirsh's words were just too much to stand. And I saw all at once that Mr. Hirsh was scared. He was scared of the baby, so he didn't want me around, even though he might want to, because it made him feel bad. He stood there showing me these magazines, and all the time I felt how tired I was of his presents and how I hated being given things and how bad it made me feel. And then I looked at Mr. Hirsh and at the cradle and paint bucket. And I knew I'd made it all up. That Mrs. Hirsh would have the baby and Bobby wouldn't even try to stop it. And I'd been afraid of Mr. Hirsh finding out, when all the time it didn't matter and I'd just been playing a stupid game with myself.

"Well, how about it?" "No thanks, Mr. Hirsh," I said, trying to smile. "You're sure?" And he held them out like he was just dying for me to take them. "I've got too much school work to read magazines," I said. "I better go up and do it too."

And sure enough, he didn't die or carry on. He wasn't even sorry to hear me go. "Ok, David, you do your work if you have to." And I walked off and left him by the table. "David!" he called when I reached the stairs. "If you want, you can help me paint this sometime." But I knew enough to know he didn't mean it, and I'd decided I didn't want to be where I wasn't wanted.

I didn't do homework; I sat by the window and waited for Bobby to come from playing with his gang. I felt good when I saw him down the street. I ran out to tell him how wrong I'd been. "Bobby," I said, "You're not gonna stop the baby." "Of course not," he said. "And I'm not gonna talk to you." "But how come—?" "Because you thought up that plan and my mother says I shouldn't." "But I'm not gonna do it." And I could see he was getting madder every minute.

"You planned it. You planned it and said it was my plan." "You'd think it up, Bobby. You liked it." "My mother said I wouldn't do that!" he yelled. "You wouldn't do it." "She said I should tell Mr. Hirsh." "No, Bobby." "And that's what I'm gonna do." "No!" "I'm gonna tell him right now." He walked off past his house and I watched him go up our driveway and through the back door.

I just stood there and walked in circles and watched it get dark. And then I went in and sat in the dark thinking what I could do. And all these bad thoughts went through my head, so I had to turn on the victrola to drown them out. I turned it on loud and tried to drift away. And all at once there was a knock on the ceiling that made me jump up all scared, as if someone was in my head. I knew it was Mr. Hirsh knocking to make me quiet, so I turned off the music, but that made me feel worse. And I didn't want to see him, but now I did all over again— and I couldn't. I kept saying to myself ok, ok. And after a while, when I was sure no one was listening, I tip-toed out the back door downstairs to the cellar. The magazines were still next to the cradle on the table. I grabbed up a bunch and locked the door behind me.

3.

I had to have something. I read the stories about pirates and ships. I brought the victrola to my room and listened to symphonies in the dark and told myself the stories over and over till I fell asleep. And then I cut out the pictures and nailed them on the walls, even when I knew I shouldn't. They were all pretty girls and cruel pirates and had names like Lady Jane and Princess Ann and Bad Sam. A few times, when the music got loud, Mr. Hirsh knocked and I turned it down. I'd look at the pictures and not feel so bad. The girls were still pretty, even Bad Sam was all right, and I could still hear the music. So I got to like my room more and more. It was mine. I wouldn't let anyone see it.

Then one night I heard the Hirshes come down the back stairs. I heard Mrs. Hirsh moaning and Mr. Hirsh saying doctor, somebody. I was perfectly still. I didn't move or breathe till they were down. Doors opened and slammed, the car started and backed down the driveway. "It's ok," I whispered. "They're not coming back. It's not real. They're not." Then I turned on the light and looked at my pictures. Lady Jane smiled and I knew she was more real than Mr. or Mrs. Hirsh "And Bobby isn't real," I whispered, and felt strange somehow. I looked out my window and there was Bobby's house. But I worked it out— it was only there when I saw it, and when I didn't see it, it wasn't there. I pulled down the shade.

That was the night I made up my own stories. I was Captain Lopez. I saved all the girls and gave pirate treasure to the poor. The next day I found a long stick and taped a piece of wood across it. And each night I made up stories and practiced sword fights with the music going and the pretty girls flashing past me.

But then came the last night when I was in bed half-asleep I heard a noise. I couldn't tell what. And then I heard it again and knew the baby was there and was crying. I tried not to hear, I covered my ears with the pillow. But I couldn't stop it, it was too loud. I turned on the light and put on the victrola, but I still could hear the baby crying. I tried to think up stories, I got up and walked around and still it was there. I got my sword and started fighting. I saw the girls on the walls and heard the baby and turned the music louder. I was Captain Lopez, Bad Sam kidnapped Lady Jane. I caught up to the pirates and swung over on a rope. I killed one and two and three— and they were all dead. There was only Bad Sam and Lady Jane, she cried for me to save her. I chased Bad Sam around the ship, around chairs over the bed. He almost got me, but I flew past him, into the closet and out. Over we went, back and forth across the bed He tripped and fell, Lady Jane smiled and cried David! David! and I leaped on Bad Sam and stabbed him through— crash! The bed fell down. Mr. Hirsh called "David!" He'd come into our house, stamped through the rooms and sprung open my door. "There's a baby upstairs!"

He stared at me over the bed posts, his face angry and red, and then he looked surprised. I was in my underwear twisted in the blankets on the mattress on the floor with the sword in my hand. I watched him see the chair and the clothes from the closet on the floor, and then my girls and pirates on my walls. Then his eyes came back at me.

"Didn't you hear me knock? What the hell you been up to?" "I stole the pictures," I said. "What?" He made a face and turned off the music. "I stole the magazines and tore the pictures out." "But I said you could have them." "I stole them. Like I stole the pink balls." "Pink balls! My kid can't sleep!" "You know. You know I want to kill him." "Kill him! Are you crazy?" "Bobby told you." "I haven't seen Bobby in weeks."

And then I knew he didn't know. Bobby hadn't told him. He'd played a trick because he hated me. But I couldn't stop, it didn't matter. I laughed and laughed. "What's with you, David? You stop it and tell me." "I wanted to stop him, tie a rope across the stairs and trip Mrs. Hirsh and— woosh!" I swished the sword over and over. "Woosh!"

"Stop it David!" He grabbed the sword and pulled me up so I was screaming in his red face. I took the balls. I lied to you and got them. I stole the pictures and nailed them up "cause I knew you'd hate it!" He shook me back and forth, the room went crazy. "Stop it! Stop it!" he shouted. "I will! I'll trip him! Woosh!" He squeezed and stopped me and threw me hard on the bed. "Now you— calm down!"

I wanted to cry but I didn't. I bit my lip and stared at him. He stared back and then he looked around the room, turning the sword in his hand and talking almost to himself. "I don't believe it. If I thought you meant all this—" He looked at me again. "No! It's crazy. You're alone too much is all. Your folks—"

And then I knew I wanted only one thing from him in the world. "Say I'm no good," I said. "Say I'm bad." "Look David." And he talked slow and mean. "I know I should maybe see you more. But I got a baby now and you're going to have to be quiet. A baby needs quiet." "Hit me!" I yelled. "Say I'm bad." "It's not for me to do!" "The cradle's old. You're too old."

"All right," he said, and his face got tighter and redder than ever. "All right." His hands shook and he saw he was holding the sword, and he smashed it over his knee. "I'm old and you're bad!"

I felt faint and dizzy, as though I was light floating round and round. And I could see how glad he was to say what he said and not to have to worry about me anymore. And I was even sorry for him, because I knew he knew what it meant . . . But then he did something I didn't count on. He did it and made everything terrible forever.

"I'm gonna tear down these pictures," he whispered. And he went along the walls ripping them off and tearing them. "No, Mr. Hirsh— please!" I grabbed onto his legs and tried to stop them. "Don't do it. Hit me, but don't do it!" He dragged me along on my knees till I couldn't hold on. I sprawled on the floor and watched him tear them down till there weren't any left. "There," he said. "And don't you put up any new ones."

I wanted to say something, to tell him he didn't have to do that. But I couldn't say a thing. I looked at his face— flushed full of pain and anger— and I heard his words smash in my head.

"I'll be watching, so don't you put up any pictures or run around the room or play that damned music. I got a baby to take care of— yeah, and not much time. So don't you make her cry again— or do anything, or I'll make you wish you hadn't. You hear? You be quiet or I'll fix you good."

He turned his back and left the room. I stayed put till I heard him on the stairs and then I got up and shut my door. I threw the pictures and pieces of wood in the basket and yanked out the nails. I picked up the chair and clothes; I worked the mattress till I got it back up. Then I straightened the blankets and got in bed. I could see holes in the walls from the nails. And upstairs I could hear the baby screaming and the Hirshes talking. And I knew even then they'd always be there. And Mr. Hirsh would always watch me, he'd watch me and warn me and never let me forget. And if I put up pictures he'd tear them down. And if I played music loud, he'd knock on the ceiling and I'd remember. And I tried to think of something new, someone, but I was scared to. And I knew if he'd hit me, it would have been better. But now I couldn't stop till I made him hit me — and I knew he never would. I leaned out of bed and pulled over the basket and found Lady Jane. She was all crumpled up and torn— only half there, one eye gone. And I kissed her goodbye and I cried.

I lay still in bed and cried inside me. And I thought of the pirates inside and my room, and about when I was Sid Gordon. And then I saw Bobby. He had a mask. He climbed, he tied the rope across the stairs. Mrs. Hirsh screamed, David! And then I knew I was every one; the Hirshes screaming for help, Bobby slashing with his knife— and even Mr. Hirsh's baby dying in Mrs. Hirsh's stomach. And all the time I was the boy who lived downstairs.

ONE WAY TO CALIFORNIA

1.

Let me tell you about my father— or at least how my father got to California.

First you should know that he got there in a deluxe 57 Cadillac, long and black, with those arched and flashing fins gliding out on a road straight to heaven. Power steering, power brakes, electric windows, twin headlights, remote control aerial, AM/FM, stereo speakers—the works, as they'd say in those days. The works, except for one thing: it wasn't air-conditioned. That's what he took or what took him to California. And I've already told you one reason why he went.

My father always thought big, dreamed big. His big thinking led him to over-stock his over-big, debt-ridden restaurant, only half of which was his, and caused him to travel with the Big Men—which meant big gin rummy games, big bookie tabs and therefore big payoffs of big money, less than half of which was his. The rest of the cash he took on the sly from the till, or, what soon proved easier, from banks. Since the one he "borrowed" from was his own brother, he didn't go to jail.

My mother could never figure out, and my father never told her, exactly what the money was for, or why the banks in Jersey always gave him credit on the business, even without his brother's signature and even after they were told to desist from so doing. But the bad debts, for all their mystery, had to be paid. And that was my mother's job. That is, she worked, hovering over the grey metal cash register, keeping my father's hands out as best she could, while the wives and mistresses of the *really* Big Men dangled their feet over the sides of Miami Beach swimming pools.

Finally, though, after nine years of evasions, the debts caught up with my father. My uncle had torn at his hair for years; his wife pointed to the peeling plaster of their ceiling, the belittled opportunities for their children; and now, most of his hair gone and the rest graying rapidly, his wife embittered and his big brother's big image shattered forever, he said, more as an epitaph than as an ultimatum, it's either you or me, Sam.

This story has to do with my father's reaction to his brother's words, with what he did, with what happened to him. So I guess I should be more careful in telling you what led to that reaction. But I have to warn you, that I can only imagine what he thought and how he felt. Because he never told me any of this, hardly a word. Some of it I know from what my sister said, or what my mother said in one unguarded moment or another over many years. But he never told me much of it, hardly anything. He would die with the story untold, and I can only try to piece it together.

Of course, the story, told this way, may well be untrue—at least in one way or another. But that's probably the case of most stories, and the story may be worth telling anyway.

2.

There are some things you should know. At age 50, my father was a 320-pound glandular monstrosity. He was bald with a nose that projected beyond his puffed cheeks like the hooked beak of a stuffed and stymied bird. His eyes were toned by heavy, half-closed lids. The flaccid, yellowing jowls, the cynically humorous curve to his thick lips made his face a mask.

His body was gutted by infirmities of all kinds. A calcium deficiency blotched his hands brown; warts rose like bangles on his neck and trunk. He had sciatica, a bad back, some inexplicable illness that shot up from spine or spleen and skewed his left eye; he had diabetes, an ulcer and worst of all, kidneys that produced crystals and stopped and tore at his urinary track about twice a year, assaulting and racking his body, and (what finally did him in) taking its toll on his initially strong and intractable heart. All his diseases cut into the things he could eat, and all his disease-geared diets clashed. This was the price he paid, the product of a process—all for being who and what he was and what being all that made him want to be or do. In the end, aging, wilting and heading toward death in the California sun, he would not feel so big. Ills and pills would not leave him so big either.

But before, in his Jersey salad days, he'd gone about his business like two workaholics and two hedonists trapped in the same body. It must've seemed to him like all his Jewish buddies had made it big during the war, even as the oh-so-chosen people were being hounded and murdered in Europe. In the 1950s, he found himself playing that desperate game of catch-up where you only see the ones who are ahead, and where they've already got such a leg up on you that they only moved further into the lead the harder you ran. Life meant work, work meant success, success meant consuming, consuming meant life as much as things. So he worked sixteen hours a day and then danced Latin music like a bloated Astaire and then played cards (disastrously) much of the night.

The only way I can account for all that raw energy is by thinking of the way he must have seen those around him and then, after all was said and done, by chalking it up to stubbornness and will. Enough of both he had for certain. Where he got them Yahweh only knows, but they were deeper and greater than I have seen in any other man. Deeper and greater and maybe more wasted.

There was that night at Roosevelt Raceway, when he'd gone to the bathroom three breaks running. At first I thought nothing of it. We were supposed to be partners betting out of a joint pool. But he always wandered off, and never really tried to hide the fact that he was placing some pretty hefty side-bets of his own. (He only let me know directly when he won and wanted to cover some losses of our dipping pool funds.) But after the second time, I began to feel his tension—I saw that hardening at his mouth corners: one of the few facial expressions he could muster. After the fourth race, I saw him grit his teeth and press his lips together. He sweated and squinted, his eyes watered. Dad, I said, let's get out of here. But he wouldn't go, he had Big Money on the fifth race, and he was going to stick it out, even though we both knew by now what was coming on him.

Well, he lost the fifth, but won the sixth and only let me get him to the car after he'd stood in line to collect his winnings. All the way home from Long Island, I heard his sighs, his choked gasps and groans, as he spasmed and flailed in the back seat.

I had to ward off his arm flings, his fists pounding on windows and cushions. I crimped my neck and clutched the wheel, tearing down the long highway, across Manhattan to the Tunnel, and then along the Turnpike, and home. Finally we made it to the apartment complex parking lot. I jostled and pried him, a wobbling, unmanageable dead-weight mass, out of the car and up the walk; I stuffed him through the door and into the house, cleared off his blankets and prepared to push him onto his bed.

But before he went down, he gave me a smile out from below some six levels of pain and misery, and handed over a bloody kidney stone the size of a marble.

Such was his stubbornness, his will, his pride, his way. This is what he brought to the big race that was his life.

3.

I suppose that when it's important for you to think people think you're important or special, then you've got to be or do or get what it is that would make you feel you've created the needed illusion. If you'd met my father, you'd have been repelled or embarrassed at first; but the feeling wouldn't have lasted for long. At the deep center of his bloated mass his will sent out yeah-saying signals, life-affirming bleeps in the fog. So he came to have his famous assets: his extravagant generosity ("always tip big, son, never let them think you're cheap"), and while we saw little of them at home, where his "little problem" made everything he said and did sputter and die like so many wet firecrackers, a great sense of compassion and humility (he had plenty of both), and a notoriously "fabulous" sense of humor (this joined with a memory for jokes and a knack for telling them)—all in all, the neat package of traits which added up to be what they used to call "a real mensch."

The fact is, my father had all the assets but one. My father lived in America the Beautiful, but he didn't have money.

It's hard to write about money especially if you're trying to deal with your father, and when you're not really sure what your writing could mean as you try to imagine what your father thought and wanted, without really knowing if that's the way it was. I have trouble accepting the fact that this man who left me so troubled, had unknowingly bartered his every smile or tear, every lift of eye or finger, each damned flick of every cigar ash, to win the people and do the things he thought he had to do, to bring him the stash of cash that was to ever elude him any way.

His own mother had preserved the gentility she had nurtured as a seamstress (or tailor's aid) in the Tsar's court; but his father had maintained the brutal ways he'd learned as commissary provisioner in the Tsar's army. He was one of those Jews who made himself valuable to his bosses—in his case by entering peasant villages ahead of the troops to terrorize the peasants into offering up their wines and meats, their cheeses and chickens, and maybe their daughters too. He must have felt betrayed by the pogroms, and he took his wife and infant child (my father) and came to the U.S., bypassing the New York City Jewish ghetto as fast as he could, taking whatever route available in those days to get to New Jersey and enter the U.S.A. for real.

But how could the man ever expect to fit in the community where he lived? What kind of Jews were these who hardly spoke a word of Yiddish? What kind of Jew was that, so crude and foul-tongued and hard-drinking? Whoever heard of a Jewish drunk? Unable to hold a job, he drifted from business to business, never getting anywhere. He abused his wife, his oldest son and then others of his growing brood. My father dropped out of school early to support his mother, his brothers and his sister. The aging patriarch became a pariah in the community; he drifted in and out of the house, gone for days at a time, turning harsher and more bitter with each passing month. Perhaps a killer of peasants in the Old World, he became known to curse his own people and wish them dead when he had a few drinks. He grew to hate every one, above all himself. One cold morning in 1936, the Great Depression and he too now in the deepest funk, he stuck his head in the gas oven and killed himself. However loveless and harsh their marriage, his long-suffering wife, my father's mother, (maybe out of despair, maybe out of joy, who knows?) died the very next day.

I was born only three years later, my life perhaps an answer to their death. But my father never once told me about them, never once brought them up, skirted the subject if I or some one else mentioned them. At least outwardly, he had so cut off himself from the mainsprings of his life, that I have only been able to piece them together after who knows how many years of living and asking. This story is another stage of the piecing together, the work of some one still trying to understand his father's past, to make sense of his own past and future, and whatever meaning they might be said to have on this planet.

Can we see it all in a nutshell—or through a glass ever so darkly? Born of a family alienated from its own community, my father sought to become a community pillar. Given the fact that he never became rich, he did pretty damn well. He was a founder and first president of his synagogue, became a 32nd degree Mason, a Shriner and who knows what else. But he started with problems and he never could overcome them. The eldest son, he had borne the brunt of his father's failures and violence, and long before he'd accepted full responsibility for his brothers and sister, carrying them on his shoulders, dropping out of the seventh grade, selling newspapers and then working in the deli-business, helping each one of them to get started in his kind of work. He was still helping them, struggling out of the muck, when the depression hit another big snag and pushed him so far down, he couldn't fully get up even with the war.

Then, as what was happening happened in the old world, many of the new world Jews amassed their stakes, and, by hook and at least a fair number by crook, catapulted themselves into the established and ever-upward bound middle class and even beyond. All around him, friends and relatives were making it— and there was even the case of his Communist butcher (and concert singer) cousin, who tried desperately to hold onto his politics even after he had made a million because of special wartime meat deals his wife handled while, a CP-United Front enlistee private, he peeled potatoes in a local camp waiting for a chance to fight the Nazis that never came. Coming out of the war, realizing how much his wife had made, he tried to give the bulk of his money to help rebuild the Soviet Union. His wife didn't quite agree, keeping control over the money, sending their kids to private schools and universities, buying a lifetime Jewish country club membership, and sending letters to the *NewYork Daily News* explaining how and why loyalty to her adopted country led a good, patriotic Jewish woman like herself to express her outrage against the Rosenbergs and her not too oh-so-reluctant support for their execution. Meanwhile her husband, confused by his new wealth, his fancy new home and well-educated children he increasingly couldn't understand, spent his dwindling days listening to the classical music albums he so loved, inviting over my father and other cousins (my uncles, but not the one he would sometimes rob—that one had to stay at the restaurant) so they could play gin rummy like in the good old days, while I sat in the next room, hearing those great classical albums, those sublime and vulgar Wagnerian swoops and swoons of *Furtwängler* conducting Kirsten Flagstad (I remember one uncle— best known for his Nat King Cole imitations, shouting, how can you let the boy listen to those Nazis?). But there I sat drenched in great music while the men slammed down their cards and I dreamed of another world, another life—until it was time for the Friday night Gillette boxing matches, time for the brown bomber, Sugar Ray, Rocky Graziano, Jake Lamota, Willie Pep, Kid Gavilan (what a bolo punch) and not one new Jew in the whole bunch.

In the war's aftermath, now in his forties, my father made the desperate plunge to break out of oblivion, to catch up with friends and relatives and taste the fruits of cash and success. But they began moving out of the neighborhood, when he didn't; their kids started going to Ivy League schools , while his own daughter had to spell her mother at the cash register and go to a third rate college, until she dropped out, got married and moved to California to escape it all. And meanwhile his one and only beloved boychick got turned down by all the rich girls who no longer lived in the neighborhood, and had to ride his rocking horse to pick trotters and pacers to fund one, but only one, year, at a second level ivy league college before my father and mother and then yours truly followed my sister into exile, where, realizing there was no money and also that my beloved father was either a smalltime crook or at least a reckless gamer intent on ruining us all, I ended up going to a commuter state u. while I took on one part-time job after another just to barely graduate on one fine day and write this story on another one.

I don't doubt for a minute that my father justified all his mad, mindless maneuvers to avoid exactly what happened to my sister and me. But starting late and without all the advantages, my father only went so far; and by the definitions he accepted, failed. Failing, he had to give the appearance of success, find ways to get to Miami and (the best) Havana, buy his wife a mink—get all the outward signs of something that wasn't. So it was that he got involved with bankers, loan sharks, bookies and other assorted Mafia small fry. So it was that somewhere between his good intentions and his actions, money had stuck up its giant head. He'd become caught up in it—its ups and downs, its actions and transactions. So what came to be the story of my father was the story of money—the ways he tried to get it and spend it, and the ways it got and spent him and us.

4.

My father had to be big, a big giver, a big tipper—always with a wad in his pocket, a cigar in his mouth, even if he choked on it. He had to go to the "classy" places and pick up the tab. Working long hours every day, mixing with men who paraded their new wealth, he nurtured desperate dreams of sudden wealth, of heaps of money that would end his miserable and shameful obscurity. In other men, he was sharp enough to detect this madness and scorn it. In himself, he denied its existence and yet it lived. But in some funny, frustrating way: he could not smash his fetters completely, and so he never robbed a bank or stormed the mint. Instead, he cheated his brother and wife.

The first time he took money, it must have hurt him. But the very fact that he was a "feeling man" made it impossible for him to live with a burden of guilt. Basically he wanted to continue living as he felt compelled to and still maintain a good opinion of himself. So, when he took the money he must've said, this is the one and only time. And since he had lived through the first confrontation by the family, the second had to be a little easier. Of course, he was a man who dreaded condemnation far more than he dreaded stealing. And when, after a while, the confrontations became insufferable, he became a man avoiding the future, disappointed looks and scandalized accusations. For years, he played a cat-and-mouse game of paying off old debts by contracting new, of staving off his wife's discoveries by means of constant concealment and lies—all fronted by a bravura show that was designed to be "winning."

By the time his oldest debts were uncovered, it was easy not to feel guilty—they were so much part of a distanced past. Besides, a man gets tired of recriminations and regret; and if he finds a need to continue with their causes, he'll invent deceits to shield himself. If my father had been unable to believe his own lies and rationalizations, he would have been unable to carry the burden.

Over the years, he began to see his good opinion reflected by those around him—his big friends, and some of the lesser lights who frequented his restaurant. He was the grand host, the big sport, the swell guy. He had gradually sacrificed the respect of those closest to him. And when he could no longer see admiration written on their faces, he no longer relied on them to keep himself afloat.

There are some funny things involved here. By definition, my father had to be a "fine family man," one who thrived on intimacy, the home as refuge and the rest of it. He was a bright man, one who could be sensitive to others. He secretly prided himself on his ability not only with words but with paint, music, plants and just about everything. He was after all an artist of roasts and coleslaw and *hors d'huerves* trays—a master caterer like a master of theater. But he had long learned to regard his family and artistic sides as just trimmings, to be put aside with a sadness what was at least somewhat feigned. And so, in spite of the phoniness that was part of the package he had bought, you couldn't help but feel that he was one of those who were trapped into performing a role he was never meant to play.

I mean when you think about everything that went into his performances, and if you can somehow separate what his questionable acts (and you can't do it, I know) from the ends he hoped they would serve—when you think how he had succumbed to things, when you realize he didn't have any one he could level with for fear of exposure—then you realize how some of his best values and qualities had become terribly twisted and had turned against him. None of this is to excuse him. No, in the midst of all the circumstances and determinants, he had chosen. Somehow all his best impulses had become warped and had bred serpents. By an act of love—for his family, for his community, for himself—he had early fitted himself into a life he could never long conform to, and, never completely break with. Like other American Jews of his time and situation, he was on the road to "setting in"—and if he couldn't do it by hook, he'd do it by crook.

5.

So when my uncle finally held his breath and said what he had had to say for years on end, my father's reaction had to have been worthy of the complex man that he was. Don't get the idea that he was completely callous. No doubt he regretted all the sorrow he had caused, the bills that could only be met through the sacrifice of some one else. The nine years of work that had been reduced to pathetic absurdity because of his "little weakness." Perhaps he realized that his brother had had to play the failure to his own wife and kids to cover for what my father was doing. Surely he regretted that his wife viewed him with contempt, that because of his actions, she'd been forced to take control of all his affairs, making him accountable to her even for his cigar money.

But how much regretting can a man do? My father was a complex man, and he could go beyond callousness. He could say that whatever he'd done, he done it hoping his family would benefit. He could justify himself for the sake of his son's future. He could blame business problems on his brother's and wife's imagination not matching his own. In business and marriage, he could argue, that he had heavy, unwieldy weights around his neck. Wasn't he smarter than both of them, and hadn't he worked hard for years and years only to have to it all brought to naught through their constant interference? If he hadn't had the guts and know-how to win himself friends—big, substantial men according to any one's standards—wouldn't his only leisure hours have been dominated by his wife's canasta clique or his brother's petty-anti, penny-a-point card playing friends—small timers all?

He could point to the dreams he'd had as a boy—dreams that had been thwarted because certainly his father wouldn't heed the hungry yelps of his brothers and sisters. Hadn't he earned a little slack for keeping his family alive, for helping his brothers get started, for being able to support their own families at all? Hadn't he sacrificed his own education, the very possibilities of his life? Was he meant to be no more than a food peddler? Didn't he have all kinds of potentials that out of love and duty he had been unable to develop? Hadn't every Lions Club in Hudson County gone out of their way to invite him as their after-dinner speaker? Hadn't his fellow religionists honored him for his service and sacrifice? All his lofty dreams he'd given up to peddle newspapers at 5 a.m. and in a deli until 10 p.m. And for what? For a brother with no sense of foresight, no sense of bigness and no ... no gratitude.

For having taught his brother everything he knew about the food business, having given much of his life to others, wasn't he not now entitled to some simple pleasures? Was his whole life to be one great sacrifice? Didn't he have any rights? Oh, it was true he hadn't counted on having to milk the business. How'd he know the bookies'd be at his throat? He had to take the money—yes. But he swore to pay it back. Certainly he never thought he'd have to borrow again and again. But the debts were being paid, weren't they? And after all he'd done for his brother, so what if it hurt a little?

And as for my mother, well didn't he love her as a man should love his wife? And it wasn't that she was the most brilliant woman in the history of the world, either or the most beautiful, if you really wanted to know. Not that he didn't appreciate her, far be it from him not to. But hadn't she gotten ample reward by being able to lord it over him—being able to call the shots with someone for the first time in her life? And her always nagging him for being overweight. Sam, you're getting too fat. Sam, don't sit down and rip your pants. Sam, don't stick your hands in your pockets. As if his weight made any difference. As if eating wasn't after all an occupational hazard he had to live with. And, yes, maybe even a sign of affluence and ethnic pride. As if they held a monopoly on being right and good. As far as he could see, the whole thing was unfortunate, but it was obvious to any man of insight who the real victim was.

Worse than callous, my father was foolish and self-deluded. His first resulting rationalization was a crude one: I'll leave my brother with this heart breaker of a business. He had certainly caused enough trouble, let's see if he can take it. Basically a generous man, however, he found no satisfaction in this formulation. And so he fashioned for himself a set of logical imperatives that enabled him to triumph. *Desperate smugness*: my brother is uncooperative; *disdain*: he's ungrateful; *self-pity*: I've always loved my brother; *triumphant*: I forgive my brother.

Thus it became an act of great magnanimity for him to hide his brother's baleful blame. Of course, knowing what he knew, he couldn't stay in the business. He forgave his brother, of course, but that didn't mean he had to continue taking unnecessary abuse. Better to leave while they were still on good terms. End in a businesslike, amicable manner. So he came to believe it was time to get out of an unfortunate trap. He convinced himself that he was tired of accusations and of work that was fruitless. He told himself—and then his friends—that when a man in his position, who had worked so hard and so long, was past the age of fifty, it was the moment to stop the merry-go-round, to get off and start relaxing and enjoying life while there was still time. No, he wasn't going to retire—my mother was quick to remind him that this was impossible—and he told his friends that of course a man like himself couldn't be completely inactive. He would move to a pleasant, warm climate, and work maybe a few hours a day and just—just take it easy.

6.

And where was this retiring magnate going to settle? But there could be no question about it—at least not to my father. Where were most of his friends going to live? Where is a successful first generation American Jew (of good will) supposed to live?

But my mother didn't like the idea of Miami Beach. My father knew too many people there to gamble with and borrow from. Besides, she reminded him, you're going to have to work. And not just to fill his leisure hours either. Miami Beach wasn't the place for a man his age to get a job. Don't be silly, he said. And in his mind you could see he expected a good two hundred thousand from the business. No (the dream blossomed), two hundred fifty, three hundred thousand. And he said it.

My mother had grown haggard from trying to understand him, from living day to day not knowing when he'd do some terrible thing next; she'd become bitter and sharp-tongued. You're crazy! Absolutely out of your head! We'll be lucky to get seventy-five thousand. Of course this was absurd. But he thought he'd try another tack—the martyr. Well, what do you want me to do? Tell me. I'll go to Scranton and work in a coal mine if that's what you want. No! She insisted. To California! To their daughter and grandchildren. At least there he stood half a chance to get a job; there they needed men who could cut a corned beef or make a potato salad that tasted just right; there she'd at least have her daughter who'd care about her, to say nothing about taking her side (for who thought anything about her here: *Sylvia-the-hag, Sylvia-the-drag, Sylvia-the-nag,*

Sylvia-now-Sam-this-or-that) if he should wind up pulling his old stunts again.

They'd been to California on visits for recent summer vacations, even though it had meant not being able to afford winters with his friends in Miami. It wasn't that he didn't like the West Coast, mind you (could his daughter or his son-in-law make a bad move?). The future was in California, no doubt about it. But California was not his cup of tea. California was only second best. A man in his position *had* to go to

Miami. Why I don't think he knew precisely. Maybe he saw California as orange trees mowed over by asphalt and iron, as the speed and force of the future, young, hard and ruthless, and not the golf and sun of a leisure well-earned. Whatever the reason, he knew her estimate of their business share was way below the mark, so he told her they'd wait and decide after the selling terms were settled. And meanwhile he told his well-meaning friends he was Miami-bound.

7.

It was his estimate that proved absurd as he found out on a day in early March when he walked with confidence and indeed a kind of benign arrogance into the accountant's office and just minutes later walked out, his future place in life all but determined.

The substance of the meeting went something like this. The accountant figured the business was worth $165,000. My father groaned: the business was worth way over $400,000, and the accountant was in it with his brother or some one to rob him of his due. But what you don't seem to understand, Sam, is that the business owes. Well sure it owes, but—... It owes about 150 grand--including a good chunk to banks for various unaccountable transactions, the accountant added, fairly glaring, and then turning away, taking off his horn rims and wiping them with a piece of torn tissue.

My father grumbled, but held his peace; he grumbled once more and more deeply when he found his share set at $53,000. Politely, the accountant hid certain miscellaneous embezzlements behind a mendacious statement claiming that my uncle's initial investment exceeded my father's by so many thousands. Thus history received the kind of sugar-coating we've since learned to associate with the crimes of Stalin or the Watergate.

Of course, my father had his own version of the story. He was appalled at the colossal ingratitude. In his heart he thought he'd been swindled. But he was a big man. And though he saw his life getting a jolt (if not the shaft) and though the prospect of some grim future days began to loom before him, he made no scene. In effect, it was not his style; it did not become a big man to whine or wheedle or wheeze, and so... he said nothing.

He said nothing and did nothing, even when they worked out terms that were far from inspiring. First, they were to receive $5,000 in cash. The rest was to be paid off in monthly installments of $500 over the next eight years while they sought to establish themselves in their new life. He knew all too well it was peanuts, a deal geared strictly geared to the tax structure. But he knew that because of his finagling, the business could afford no other arrangement. All the years, all the work and just six thousand coming in each year so my uncle and his family could begin to live a life. The whole thing was chicken shit, and he knew it. But still he said nothing, did nothing. And then again, what was there to say or do?

You see, I think there was more to my father's silence than his being above it all. I think that for all his swagger and ability to fool himself, he'd had some inkling into the outcome of this meeting. I mean $250, 300 thousand had been another one of his desperate dreams of sudden heaps of money. He'd tried to make himself believe his estimate by recklessly boasting of his semi-retirement in Miami. Perhaps he'd hoped he could will it into reality. But he'd never completely believed it. And when he was confronted ever so gently, all he could do was feel that the world had collapsed on him. All those years, all the work come to so little because of some small defect, some lapse, some small problem—the kind of problem any big man could have. Groggily, on pure instinct learned from years of seeking appreciation, he smiled, signed the papers and said good-bye. All his will could do was improvise some weak little lies that would absolve him of responsibility. Make him triumphant his will could no longer seem to manage.

8.

The picture I get of my father's last months in New Jersey is of a man being forced out of what had actually been his life—of what, for better or worse, he'd sold his first beautiful dreams for. True, he'd cheated his business, crippled it while it was growing—but he'd worked, sweated and given his all in trying to make his lies realities. Defeated, he urged himself not to admit defeat. He wasn't going to be pushed out, he was retiring. His friends told him he was doing a wise thing. They patted him on the back. And so he even came to believe he was doing a wise thing—something only a big man could do. Everything was fine, the standard operation he was used to performing—except for one small detail. This time, he couldn't quite believe it. Almost, but not quite.

The reasons aren't hard to come by. Age was one thing. For a good part of over fifty years, he had carried his 320-pound bag of trouble around his bones. He'd had sickness after sickness. He'd been pierced by more needles, regulated by more conflicting pills and diets than any six sickly men. He'd made move after move that he'd had to make palatable. He'd had secret upon secret that he'd had to conceal by using every ruse he had at his command. Time was heavy on him. His fringe of hair was near white. His spindly legs felt the weight of his huge belly. Perhaps his will had been declining for years without his knowing. And the sudden change of circumstances, the change of horizons, of fears, of things to cover up had merely made the decline a little obvious.

Perhaps, if nothing had changed—if my uncle hadn't taken that deep breath and finally said he'd had to say—my father's will could have trudged along out of force of habit, and he could have gone on for who knows how long?

As it was, for the first time in years, my father had the chance and overt need to sit down and consider his future. And with the tired, leaden weight of his past, he saw all the things he had to do: all the countless goodbyes, the trip, the fuss to make new friends, the efforts required to start out all over again. And in an instant something inside him doubted his abilities and said, I can't do it, I'm too tired. And maybe in that instant he'd grown old.

The point is not that his will was dead; it was declining. It was becoming harder for him to shield himself from a heaviness and darkness of heart, harder for him to forget his actions, harder for him to maintain a good opinion of himself. Not that he couldn't rise to an occasion. He could and would for some time to come. It was just harder. And he couldn't sustain illusions long enough to fully turn apparent failures into triumphs. And having, in an instant, unconsciously doubted his will, he was no longer able to reject confusing, self-incriminating questions. He became lost in a maze of doubts, of cross-purposes, of regrets. Thus he imposed a double labor on his will. He aided, sped his own decline.

Desperately he tried to live as if he were as strong as ever. But with his gradual, slight, ever-imperceptible decline, he lost the ability to adapt, to change his manner of living, even as he planned to change most radically. He continued to fabricate lies when he could no longer feel guiltless for them. Nor could he still always construct them with the same ruthless logic. As he grew more desperate, as he doubted himself more, he exaggerated, made his lies bizarre, fantastic. He built huge castles on quicksand, trying to fool himself. But though he tried and sometimes almost succeeded, he—or one part of himself— could not believe his lies. He felt ill at ease with them. He no longer had faith in them. Brooding only made it worse, created additional strain, additional self-consciousness. And when this happened, he was no longer sure that any man believed him. Perhaps all this explains his failure at the accountant's office, and why he almost broke under the series of frustrations that were soon to sour his days.

9.

Like the man says, you can go on for years in the same circumstances, doing act after act like some machine. Change your circumstance, pull the old life out from under you, and, if you've grown old, it'll show. Had my father left Jersey an hour after his unhappy interview with the accountant; had he thrown himself immediately into a new life and occupied himself with all the problems that, in his easy chair, seemed so overwhelming, the decline of his will might have been prolonged over several years. But that's not what happened—is it even thinkable? A man in his position? A hundred things had to be done before he left—a hundred crippling chores. And in the meantime, he had so many chances to brood and worry, and (because of who he was) keep everything to himself.

The first blow was that our big magnate was Miami-bound no more. He'd dreaded this, and even after the fiasco at the accountant's he'd tried to convince my mother that he could find work in Miami. But he himself knew he would need work and Miami was not the place to find it. So his protest was weak, and in the end, he yielded.

Let me try to trace the pattern of his actions in the face of this defeat. It wasn't too hard for my father to place the change of destination in a flattering light. To himself he could say—as my mother'd said, in truth, of herself) that in California at least, he was loved. To his friends, he could say that he'd thought it over and Miami seemed like a place for old men. California, now, California was new. Young blood, a new world, things to see, things to do. After all, he'd say, I don't want to get old before my time. Besides (for he was no longer sure of himself and he had to press a bit hard), he wanted to be near his daughter and her family; he wanted to help them. Not that his son-in-law wasn't doing all right—his son-in-law a failure? But he just wanted to give him the benefit of his experience.

Saying all that blather was easy enough, but something in my father made him feel it wasn't convincing. He thought he detected a touch of scorn behind the smiling, nodding heads. He even wondered: had his brother told his friends about the business settlement? He scoffed at the idea, which didn't stop it from reappearing.

The next problem was a job, and not because our magnate was used to being active. Even my frugal mother was used to living on quite a bit more than six thousand a year. And she certainly realized there had to be money for the last years after that. You get used to money, even if you can't dangle your feet over the side of a Miami Beach swimming pool. Her beloved only son was already in college, and that was costing and would continue to cost. If I was a possible ace in the hole, an investment would have to be made even if part of the deal inevitably meant my transfer to the state u. I've already told you about. (You sure it's o.k. son? he would ask, because you know we want the best for you. Sure dad, I told him.)

My father had to know my mother was a doubly worried person because on the one hand, they had to watch their money; and on the other, they had to spend it. Great wielder of words and man of good will that he was, my father told her not to worry. Lots of his pals had connections of the West Coast. He'd have no trouble getting himself a nice, comfortable job. And because he couldn't really believe this, because that old thing in him kept on saying, who'd give you a job? At your age? Obese as you are? He struck back like a scared animal. When I say "job," I don't mean a hundred dollars a week. Why, a man of his abilities, a man of his experience, could make fifty thousand a year—with ease! Doing what he didn't know—maybe restaurant consulting, maybe public relations for something or other. Why, the more he thought of it, the more leaving the restaurant seemed to be a step out of the bush leagues. And feeling he hadn't convinced her, he said, why, his friends wouldn't let him down. Herbie, and then Joe and Morrie—them and all the others—they'd work to see to it he got something big. But you've got to think beg, feel big. So immediately he went from twenty-five to fifty cent cigars. And the following week he bought three custom-made suits.

But even with the world's finest cigar in his mouth, my father decided to play it safe. After all, wasn't he a practical man? He knew his friends had all sorts of California connections. But he couldn't very well put his hat in his hands and say, I need a job. He'd have to put it to his friends more subtly, carelessly—as if it really didn't make too much difference. His first step was over a period of days to complain of restlessness, to say it was bad for a man who'd worked all his life to just sit around. Next he'd say a man like me can't sit on his fat ass. When I get to California, I'll have to get a five day a week job or else I'll go crazy. Not that he would need it, mind you. No. He was fixed for life. But if I don't do something, I'll go out of my mind inside of a couple of weeks.

A few months before, he could have pulled it off gracefully. Because he would have believed it. But now, he didn't believe—and so he doubted if they did. He'd gotten a new ball and pawed the ground. But he was afraid to make a pitch. Several times he was on the verge. But maybe he'd perceive a bit of disinterest on the part of his listener. Maybe while he was trying to marshal his courage, his friend would go off on a different tack. Maybe the phone would ring. It wasn't an easy job. Because he couldn't bring it up more than once in a given conversation. A few months earlier he could have, and gotten away with it. But now it seemed a patronizing dead giveaway. Then too, he couldn't say it out of the blue, like, by the way, Herb, you don't know any one who could get me a job in California, do you? No, his listener had to be prepared; the rhythm of the talk had to be right. It all had to be said at the right moment, in the right context, when his listener had gotten involved in the sequence of deceits. It had to be part of a flow—a logical conclusion. Ideally, it would be volunteered without direct soliciting. It would be, say Sam, I've got a friend on the West Coast who might have just the thing for you. But what were the chances of that?

So the days passed by without my father getting any definite commitments. To my mother's queries, he'd answer something vague, like everything's under control or, don't worry, things'll be all right. Then he'd smile, his lips broadening so you couldn't tell whether it was from confidence or pain. He began to harbor resentments against his friends: they didn't give a damn when a man was down. But he couldn't say he was down, and that just showed you what kinds of friends they were really. He lit a cigar and backed off, realizing he hadn't even asked them yet. I'm just waiting for the right moment, he told himself. And when that moment came, every one would see what kind of friends a man like him had.

But he wondered; he wondered and worried and brooded. For days he'd had the feeling that his friends were getting tired of his hedging; that they knew what he wanted, but weren't interested. He was tired of trying to answer my mother, of trying to cook up excuses and only managing vague evasions. Time was dragging. The recklessness he had imagined in his scheme had become real. And even though he was full of dread about leaving, he wanted to go as soon as possible.

But there were so many things to be done. My mother was busy selling household odds and ends, getting different storage and shipment prices for her precious antiqued furniture which she loved and my father called junk. He urged her to hurry. She tried to explain, Sam, you can't just pick up and leave like a gypsy. Besides, he didn't have any definite commitments about jobs yet. Without understanding, he accepted it. He wedged himself into his easy chair. And as if he didn't have enough to worry about already, the life he brooded over gave him another swift kick.

10.

Sam, my mother said, now we're starting a new life in California. I don't want you to deep things from me any more. Now, we want a fresh start, so if there's any old debts, anything we haven't paid for yet, let me know now so we can take care of it and get it out of the way. He said there was nothing. Now I won't get mad if there is, she guaranteed. But let's start with the slate clean. I don't want to have to start paying when we first get to California.

Again he assured her there was nothing. He swore to God. And she dropped the matter for a time, only to bring it up again and again—haunt him with it. The funny thing was, he didn't really know. He'd played his cat-and-mouse game so long and so well that even he had lost track of his debts. He'd never bothered to straighten them out. If there was a way to find out it was at the restaurant. But that, he reflected sadly, was no longer his. Besides, he couldn't make a move that would arouse suspicion. Fact is, had my mother not brought them up, had, instead, my father uncovered unpaid debts of his own, he'd have probably handed them over to her without qualms and said, not without a touch of nobility, here, dear, so we can clean the deck, so when we get to California we can start fresh. But alerted in this manner, my father was determined to find out if he had debts and, if so, hide them for as long as possible. With my mother hounding him, it preyed on his mind, gnawed at his brain—if only he knew, if only he'd thought of it before! One thing he did know: if there were debts, whoever held the papers knew he was leaving; and before he left for California, the bills would come in the mail.

So began my father's first period of *Waiting for the Postman.* I know of two other such times, both in California. One over a similar, related matter and the other over letters friends never had time to write. The most striking thing about all three of these periods was that my father no longer had even the faintest illusion of freedom. He was regulated by the local delivery schedule, the postal employees, the Post Master General. The most tyrannical masters were my mother and time itself. My father had to watch his every move. He couldn't let my mother suspect he was waiting for something. He couldn't stare out the window waiting or run helter-skelter to the mailbox. Yet he couldn't let her go; nor could he protest if she did. And so his mornings were spent in a kind of dull, grinding terror until he had his paws clutched around the daily mail.

Then there were minutes of elation when what he dreaded wasn't there. But gradually, as the hours passed, the clouds would darken. Fear would grow, getting worse all the time throughout the day. Probably sometimes during the restless, troubled nights, he'd feel like talking to some one or even praying. At times you could hear him tiptoeing out of the bedroom and into the living room, where if I went to check on him, he'd quick pick up a book and pretend to be reading. But that's just the way it was the first couple of weeks. After that it got worse. I've come to the conclusion that dread and terror gave way to something new, something more insidious and pernicious: hope. Hope that what had to happen would, and soon. As a man cannot live with regret, so he cannot live with constant dread. He must give way until he practically begs doom to fall. Sometimes he works to bring it on.

I ask myself, how could he take it all? All this strain and muffling it all—-never screaming, never letting on, somehow digesting it so he could prepare a face to meet the faces. I'm sure there were moments—there must have been—moments when he contemplated death. True he was a great actor; and when he thought of death, he must have felt himself momentarily sanctified, martyred, ennobled. But it's hard to detect the actor in yourself, and some great performers have been fooled into suicide. I do know this for sure: my father's spirits were lower than I'd ever seen them.

For a time it seemed his will had completely slacked off or deserted him. I remember a night at our apartment when a group of uncles and aunts gathered to discuss the latest disaster that had befallen my mother's rich older brother, my Uncle Abe. A nice enough guy, but weak-livered, half crazy and also pretty stupid, Abe, had been arrested for trying to pass a bum check. Abe had made a fortune as butcher, but he or maybe his family (Hell, maybe he had a mistress) always seemed to squander it away, and he was always getting into hot water. Usually they'd close him down for selling horsemeat, and his brothers would have to bring in an army of lawyers to bail him out. But this time, they'd caught him dead to rights trying to pass a bum check for an amount plenty big enough to figure as heavy felony. What was his problem, we all wondered. And where would it all lead, now that he was probably bound for prison.

This was a big family disgrace, that was for sure. And all the relatives were sitting around, eating like wolves and moaning and groaning about the whole business, with my father kind of trying to play lead voice or cantor in a Kadish-chanting chorus. I don't understand it, he said, a man like Abe, with a loving wife and such a good family... risking all their happiness and security... His voice trailed off and no one seemed to notice too much because every one was talking all at once, each with his own theory about rich and crooked Uncle Abe. But my father'd stopped, he'd made the connection. He sat in silence, his double chin sank into his chest. While in the room, the talk, the clattering of coffee cups continued.

11.

This is America. And the postman brings good news as well as bad. Though usually not all deep and lasting, when you look at it squarely. But who could hope to find essential, enduring happiness for the price of a first class stamp?

After nearly two weeks of waiting for doom in an envelope, my father received a letter that sent him on a comet, made him feel ten feet tall, and the greatest, most loved guy in the state of New Jersey. His friend Herb, who'd been off in L.A. on business, had bumped into an old crony (a nice guy, by the way, Sam, you'd like him) who'd recently moved to Southern California to take over the management of the sales division of an east coast-based distributor of what who knew or cared? And what do you think? This old crony says he's going on the road, but he'll be back in L.A. by late July, and he says for you to look him up around August 1.

Immediately my father acted as if he'd already signed an agreement—and in blood. Of course, there was no direct mention of a job, but what else could Herb mean by it? Hadn't my father hedged and hedged until there could be no doubt about what he was after? And wasn't it great of Herb to understand all that without making him come out and say it? Lately my mother'd been carping at him more than ever. The other night, she'd even said to him (in her usual calm), you're lying, Sam. You don't have any jobs lined up. Sam, you're lying! Well, she see if he was a liar now. Now that he had something definite—or almost definite, which was just as good, maybe better.

The little bit of doubt was productive because it spurred him on to create iron certainty, and forced him to forge a fantasy designed to feed his confidence. No question he had a job just waiting for him. Wouldn't he be the perfect man to help introduce an east coast product? But wasn't it just like life that when it rains it pours. Because once having lined up one job, wouldn't you know it? Another one comes your way like a ripe plum waiting to be picked?

So it was that his cousin Morrie tells him that there's an opening some sort of operation for La Something or Other Cigar company in Santa Monica. And Morrie's wife's cousin's best friend says he can set up a meeting with a key company rep that'll just about assure the sweetest little job a retiring restaurateur could ever want to have.

Now, this is a real problem, no? Just when Herb's bagged one job, another comes along. And suddenly instead of worrying to death about the grim future ahead, about the callousness of supposed friends, and even doom in an envelope, suddenly you've got to worry about not hurting your friend's feelings after he's gone out of his way. You've got to work out angles and strategies and moves to play one job offer against the other to get the best possible deal. But naturally he didn't want to be greedy, and also he didn't want to worry my mother or any one around him with all the complicated decisions a man like him had to make.

So, manly man that he was, he kept his admittedly happy source of new worries to himself, and merely told my mother that all the big offers simply showed they had nothing more to worry about in California and they should get ready to go as soon as possible. As for the debts, well, with one job or the other, he could take care of any that might surface—and my mother wouldn't mind because his job worries were over, weren't they? Besides, he almost came to believe, I don't think there are any debts. I was all worked up over nothing. With all the iron force he could muster, he hitched his wagon to the job business. He was going to believe in it no matter what. The fact that he was lulling my mother into a false sense of security failed to stop him for a moment.

Characteristically, he was quick to reinforce his fabrication all the more. All things considered, they couldn't hope to leave till the middle of June, close to three weeks away. So why don't we go up to Canada for a few days? My mother wasn't sure. All the things she had to do and him hardly helping at all. And then, how were they supposed to go? They didn't have a decent car. Which was just what he wanted her to say.

Wasn't it (for God's sake) about time they got one? You can't make it in L.A. without one, and why wait till they were there? Cars were cheaper in the east, and then they could start their new life just driving out and seeing every mile of that great country that had given them and to which they had given so much. But she was afraid. She knew what he'd always wanted. Well, after all, I'm entitled to some consideration. I let you have your way about California. She eyed him harshly. Well, I've never had a car of my own. Always a business car he shared with his brother. Aren't I entitled? I mean, a man's got to have some dignity. All right, she yielded ever so reluctantly. All right, but not exactly what you have in mind.

Then he ran down all the advantages of a Caddy. The roominess, the comfort, the sense of well being. And, he added tactfully, it'll hold up for years and still be beautiful. Why, they'd never have to get another car. And so he argued for hours saying what a fine thing it would be, what an eye-catcher. And of course, he'd need it for his job—yes, that was the ticket. He'd need it for his job. He'd be traveling and mixing with big, important men. Could he take a big man out to dinner in a Chevy? He called upon his manhood, he called upon the free enterprise system and its manifest virtues. He did verbal somersaults. And he won.

Grudgingly of course. And now without his swearing he was sure about having a job and that he had no unpaid debts; for the weeks of leisure had been costing money and she hadn't been able to save as much as she wanted.

The day after that final, deciding talk on the subject, my father went in to sign the papers for his Cadillac. For he had already chosen it. He told my mother he'd looked all over town (just window-shopping, mind you) for the best buy, and he'd bartered the man down to a reasonable price. All this was untrue. Can you imagine my father bickering over a few hundred dollars? He'd gone to the nearest dealer, seen the car he liked and put down a deposit. That was the way a big man with a big job awaiting him in California did things.

Two minor concessions my father did make. First, he wanted to pay cash, but he acquiesced and flattered my mother's silly sense of insecurity. That is, my mother did not have $7,000 to put down. So he arranged a three-year combination insurance-payment plan, which, I am sure, is recorded somewhere as, dollar for dollar, one of the most profitable transactions an insurance company ever handled. The second concession was a little harder for him to take. He'd reserved a car with air-conditioning, and this my mother would not have.

Now, a big man does not go back to a dealer and say, I've decided not to take... or even, my wife insists... But my father had to do it. And I must concede he came through ably and without too many complaints, at least at first. Later, his not having the air conditioner was to gnaw at him as the difference between himself and the truly big men.

What allure did a Caddy have in those days to all those sons and daughters of migration, immigration and exile? We're dealing with a holy mystery it would be blasphemous to violate. To my father (and probably even my mother), the Caddy was a poem, a rhapsody and in blue, a Pindaric ode to the realization of a life long struggle, a beautiful hymn to more than fifty years of epic battle... What crimes, what blood of human sacrifice underpin the most profound and sublime myths?

I will be brief and prosaic. After five days of effortless driving though Canada in the newest and perhaps best loved member of our family, my father returned home to find awaiting him in the mailbox, two bills from two different banks totaling some several thousand dollars in debts contracted six years before. In an instant, they were mere debris for a late May breeze. That night, some time after dinner, my father suffered an acute attack, the culprit being diagnosed by physicians who should know as the peptic ulcer.

12.

All the deepest shadows of my father's life fell over him during those days in the hospital as he lay in his room despondent, hardly eating, hardly reacting, a subject for concern and mystery for the hospital staff and his own family. He was tired, he looked tired. His large body groaned under the treatment it had been forced to undergo, the weight it had been forced to bear. It's clear to me that all his lies were staring him in the face.

Lying in bed, my father knew: the job story had been a postponement of the inevitable—a mere trap by which he got through his days by committing himself and at least his wife to future disappointment and pain. He healed slowly, it seemed he wouldn't heal. He had no reason to heal. He was afraid, deathly afraid of exile in a strange land. Without belief in his dreams, he was lost, at the edge of despair. Having lost belief in his dreams, he was lost, at the edge of despair. But though he saw what he'd done and who he was, he could not find a way to change. Nor could he hope to or want to. For where was he to find the resources within or without to break the bonds of a slavery that had been his only source of life and freedom? Tired, suddenly old at fifty-five, could he suddenly say, to hell with all I've been and done—I'm coming clean, I'm breaking with all the shit? And could this man who felt himself so old and defeated bear to face the astonished disillusioned stares at his confession? And having thrown over his old self, his old life, could have had the strength to make a new? Could he, after all that had happened and also, above all, after all he had come to believe and value, even find out where to begin? He felt he could not; hence he could not. And maybe it was when his despondency led him to accept this state of affairs that he began to recover. Maybe it was just at this point of resignation that he could begin the process of healing, getting off his back and out of bed, of going back into training, to play his old part in the drama which had been his life—play his part until the final curtain as best as his fading talents would allow.

Is this story an indictment, an attack? Maybe, well not even maybe. But it's not against him, never against him, great actor that he was, great trouper even in his lowest moments. No, the whole thing's about something else, but not him. How could I write against him? No matter what.

13.

The curtain came a month later, when my father finally healed. The departure date had been pushed ahead to the morning of July 1st. Those last days in Jersey whirled by in a blur of packing and farewell get-togethers. But with any break in the flow and churn of things, my father was now morose, wearily sitting in his big easy chair, just overwhelmed by life. Still recovering, he'd say when asked, and he'd strain his facial muscles into a lifeless smile. No sure job awaited him in California, my mother would find out about his debts. In the face of my mother's nervous farewell gaiety, and in the midst of beaming relatives, my father had to keep it all to himself—and smile.

But there was further twist that made it all the harder. He could take all the pain, even the inkling he had that his last years might well be lived in the knowledge of bitter failure and maybe even poverty. Maybe there was no way he could avoid all this, he was accepting it as the possible, even inevitable stream of his life, and finding ways to handle it. What did not seem acceptable, what disquieted him beyond measure was the silence of his big friends. All the time he'd been in the hospital, all the time of his convalescence, he hadn't seen any of them. Cards, yes— but nothing more. It seemed unthinkable they could forget him so quickly, write him off so effortlessly. And while he was still living among them. He wouldn't ask for a party, but not even a word of goodbye?

You see, he had to have this. With all his submission and resignation, he strangely asked for this last gift. Something in him begged for a final, perhaps meaningless affirmation. Perhaps it was the hope that he could dupe himself again. More likely, it was the rhythm of the life inside him that had to be fulfilled. The great actor had to make his final flourish. In the years of oblivion and approaching death, my father had to have the memory of a last triumph, a great moment, something epitomizing the life, or at least the dream of life that he'd led on this earth. Nevertheless, on the eve of his departure, he sat motionless and near tears; and with all the absurd possibilities that could occur to him, he asked what he'd done to divest himself of some small but somehow supreme moment of triumph.

But this is the land of ironic fairy tales, of successes that blur all failures. My father was not to be robbed of his moment, nor the big friends of their last act of good will. For while he was sitting in pained meditation, the friends gathered in the gala party room of what had been his own restaurant and prepared to give him the grand sendoff.

14.

Of course it was a little messy. Every one was to have gotten there by eight; half of them hadn't shown at nine. And the man who was to have instructed my mother to have my father at the restaurant had forgotten all about his job and gone on a pleasure junket to Havana. But what are these little things in memory? At 9:20, my father received a call telling him to come over at once. And he knew! His friends hadn't let him down. Not his friends. How foolish he'd been to doubt them. How foolish! In the nervous excitement, he put on a shirt, his shoes, a soiled tie. He brushed his narrow fringe of hair and shaved, making comic remarks like the ones he'd made in better days. All the way over to the restaurant, he rehearsed what he was going to do, rehearsed for the hundredth time the way he was going to thank them. For the last time, his will blazed as of old. He exuded confidence, joviality, bravado.

It was a party with all the trimmings, much like the ones he himself had catered for others. Hors d'heurves and spreads of all kinds, animal-shaped mayonnaised salads, and a huge gaudy tiered cake topped by the effigy of a rather obese bald-headed man, standing alongside a big, beautiful Cadillac. And below the cake, on the floor, a wide array of gifts, mysterious, wrapped in paper and ribbon all around their stupendous centerpiece: a bizarre red, white and blue plastic-boxed portable TV set.

The proceedings got under way, with the warm testimonies of those who were there, the telegrams from those unable to attend, and finally a billfold with cards conferring on my father honorary membership in the Elks, the Rotarians, the Kiwanians, the Lions and all the organizations that bespoke the glory that was New Jersey. And then finally (what they'd all been waiting for), my father, humble, overwhelmed with nostalgia and joy, acknowledged the popular clamor and launched his obligatory words of thanks.

For twenty minutes he kept them in stitches. He talked of this tailor and that rabbi and even (for wasn't he American too?) the farmer's daughter. Then he grew solemn and evoked the history of Jews in the Old World and the New. He talked of ghettos and shtetls, pogroms and concentration camps. He spoke of poor persecuted Jews barely making it to cross the seas. He spoke of pushcarts and poverty in U.S. urban centers. He spoke of rich German Jews and poor Russian Jews and even poorer other Jews. He spoke of Commie, pinko and good American Jews. He spoke of Haifetz and Einstein, of Bennie Leonard and Barney Ross, Hank Greenberg and Sid Gordon, and then, above all, the great masses of simple, honest small businessmen Jews: the ground for all the others, the salt of the earth who just tried to eke out a living for their dear ones and send their kids to college so they could in turn be a credit to their families and the country that had taken them in and given them so much. How many hardships had they endured? How many sacrifices had they made? But they'd survived the pogroms and gas chambers, they'd lived through the poverty and depression, they'd lived, survived and learned to thrive, feathering their nests, yes, but also building their synagogues, and sending their kids door to door to raise money for planting trees in the New Jewish Homeland. And sure, of course, there were still lefties and pinkos among us, but less all the time, no? And it wasn't just that we thought of our own. Who more than us knew what discrimination and persecution and extermination really were, and we'd never forget, we'd always fight against them, not just for ourselves but for all, irregardless if you were black, brown or blue. But even in this we'd remained Jews even as we'd become Americans. We'd become *Jewish Americans, American Jews* now safe from old world tyrannies, and from radical temptations, now ready to forge the future in our city's suburbs or (the true frontiersmen of our time), now claiming the place we'd earned in the sun, vanguarding that great new caravan of so many going south toward Caribbean keys or west toward Pacific palisades.

Waxing ever more poetic and prophetic, he spoke of life and death and the riches of freedom and opportunity. How wonderful it was to live in this wonderful land of ours. How wonderful to have lived at this juncture in the history of humankind. He talked of the big, fabulous times with his big, fabulous friends. And then he talked of how life—life meant hellos and goodbyes. And yet he hoped and in his heart of hearts he *knew* that this wasn't the last he'd see of his friends. He'd be taking a trip back, in a year he said, to see if Milt'd lost weight and Jake'd finally fixed his garage door. And of course, of course, he was hopeful that all of them would be making their way out to the sunshine state sooner or later and they'd be guests in his home. But (his voice darkened) perhaps—life being what it was—there would never again be the closeness they all felt at this moment. Perhaps he would never see some of them again. What is the old saying? Out of sight, out of mind? Perhaps they would forget him and all they'd done together. And his friends clamored, no! no! And then the no's trailed off. The great actor paused and lit his cigar. No, he repeated. You are right, my friends. Who could really believe that? We were a communal god-fearing people. Others broke apart and went their lonely, separate ways, lost in the sea of life. But not them, not after what they'd been through—the suffering, the hard work, the good times, the good deeds, the Israel trees, the Rosenbergs. No, friends, we shall never really part. It was just that California needed us, our people out there need us. It was our call to bring the old values of the east to the west. But that would not separate us, it would bring us together all the more--a people united by their past, united by the future. Always together, never apart, at peace with their god, at home in Israel and America, struggling together, making a better world together, now and tomorrow, for themselves and their children and their children's children, as they had done in the past, as they were doing in the present and as they would do in the future—together, forever!

A cheer, a great cheer. And then, with a tremor in his voice, a thanks from the bottom of his heart, and of course a thanks too from Sylvia and all the family and well, not goodbye, but farewell!

And what could happen next? *For He's a Jolly Good Fellow* and *Auld Lang Syne*. And then the handshakes, the hugs, the backslapping. The booming voices, the smiling faces. The tears. As he made his way to the door, even his brother embraced him and murmured, good luck Sam. And then they made their way out to his car and helped him load in the gifts. He stepped behind the wheel and waved his hand a final time.

What an impression the car made that summer evening so late at night. What bigness, what beauty. What a ship to carry a big man across his big country! Before returning inside for their final drinks, the friends stood by silently until the huge red rear lights had followed the car around the corner some three hundred yards away and out of sight.

THE UNINVITED

1.

The American couple had come up from Sicily to Rome and now, after days of almost mindless tourism in the post-Christmas cold, they retreated toward the central mountains to the town inn of the provincial capital of L'Aquila. From there they would travel the next morning to visit, unannounced, the tiny mountain Abruzzi town of Carapella del Calvzio, the birthplace of the wife's father, which, he'd said, he had fled early in the century after a fight with the local priest.

Now she, her father's daughter, lacking roots she barely sensed, connections she was hard pressed to make, had decided, recently married, however fragilely, however poorly, to fulfill the wish of her father, to whom she barely felt any tie except resentment, that, if she passed nearby, she would seek out his home town and his relatives in the rocky Abruzzi terrain.

They drank deep glowing wine and ate gamey goatmeat at the inn, marveling in the warmth of the fire but also the cold against which it fended. The next morning, taking small bags with just enough clothing for one or two days, they boarded a small bus which took them some forty minutes out along a mountain highway to the roadside post where, they had been told, they could call a cab in the town to come and pick them up. The busdriver dropped them off at the correct spot, where she indeed found the phone, dialed the number she'd been given, and with her rough and minimal Italian (though better than his hapless translations from a still primitive and limited Spanish), she asked whoever answered to have the cab come to meet them.

Snow was falling, and the ground already had a light covering, the day was deep grey, the wind with a sting. Across the highway he saw a sign announcing the town they sought with an arrow pointing up a road winding its way between rocky formations that seemed to grow taller as the road went higher. On their side, a flat bed of snow gradually led to a hill of large and precarious grey rocks jutting and somehow climbing up toward a large building, which seemed to be made or rise up out of the same stones as the hill itself—a grey, unfriendly building with shuttered windows that seemed closed to the world below and to them, and with a large cross, also of grayish stone topping its flat roof and almost lost from view among the surrounding rocky hills.

After a few minutes, a van came down the road and crossed the highway to the busstop where the couple waited. The door slid open and the couple climbed in. "Dove?" asked the young driver not more than 23 years old. "A la casa della famiglia Rienza," she said in a phrase she'd rehearsed with some care. "I am the daughter – là figlia di Francesco Rienza," she explained. "Rienza!" said the van driver, "...mia cugina." From what the husband could make out the driver had turned out to be a relative, a cousin. "My name is Manfredo," he said, tall, blonde and blue-eyed. "Son of Nina Schiavo, related to the Rienza famiglia," he added. "My father—tedesco". German," he translated, with a smile, "I never knew him." The son of a Nazi soldier under God knows what circumstances, the husband said to himself.

To be sure, Manfredo was not reluctant to explain, the Germans occupied the area and there was an infusion of blondes born in the early 40s. Apparently very cruel times, as he told it, though it was hard to make out the details. But now all was changed. Many of the young people had left the town. "Roma—tutti a Roma," he added. And many of their parents soon followed them, leaving the mountain village behind and helping to raise the kids of the young ones who'd left to live in burned out slums, only later (at least some) to find their way to the new high-rise Marshall Plan-boom apartment projects that sprang up in the fifties and that they'd already seen on their stay in the city. And meanwhile those who stayed in the village continued to barely scrimp out a living, suffering through the harsh winters, herding goats, gathering and cutting wood, making do whatever way they could, with the help, one might surmise, of whatever monies those who'd gone off to Roma could send.

"And you?" asked the husband. "Where did you learn English?" "I didn't go to Roma," he said, "I go to live in New York two years with a friend," he said cheerfully. "Traveled all around, but couldn't dig in," he said, laughing. "So I came back here to help try to save our town. I'm the taxi and English interpreter. I can be your guide, if you wish!" he said cheerfully. "Maybe his name should be Virgilio," thought the husband, looking out the window at the bleak and rocky hills.

As they approached the walls of the town, Manfredo pointed to a wire suspended from a tree-like pole. "Elettricità!" he exclaimed. "Due settimane," he continued. Apparently the town had won electric power just a fortnight before their arrival. And now for the crowning touch, thought the husband, as the van made its way to the central plaza, where a few old men sat talking in the cold, and a few women seemed to be trying to warm foods to sell or eat as soon as possible.

Without much ado, Manfredo introduced them around. "La piazza," he said. "The cathedral, the town hall. The elders," he laughed. "La figlia di Francesco Rienza!" he shouted to all who might hear. "E il suo marito Americano. La figlia non parla italiano! Ha dimenticato tutto," he explained. "Non parla niente!" Which didn't prevent people from coming forward and gawking at them, even touching her coat and her hair. "Bella donna, la figlia di Francesco!" She managed an uncomfortable smile and as if to distract them, said "Look —vedere!" she exclaimed, taking out a photo from her purse. "Mi papá!" she said. There he was not too much older than he when he had left the town. "Show them this picture first of all," he said in his goodbye to the couple, giving them this and other photos to take to his home town. "Suo papà!" said one old man. "Francesco…" said another. "Fotografia vecchia," he heard, "Ma sì, Francesco,—con questa faccia dura—è proprio il figlio di Don Lorenzo Rienza." "He says, yes, it looks like Francesco, because he has the hard face of his father." And then he began rattling off a story, which she didn't grasp. "He says your father was a rebel," Manfredo explained. And now the rebel's daughter's come for a visit, the husband thought, wondering where all this might lead as the snow continued to fall without pause.

The men began talking among themselves and became very animated, almost violent in their gestural language, but it was hard to make out a word. "They talking about when he leave—they say the priest is very upset with him, they don't know why."

"Yes," that's what he told me—he said the priest threw stones at him, and he decided to leave forever."

"They say, he never wrote a word to any one, didn't come back to bury his parents, never sent them a cent."

"He was poor," she protested, "He fought in the war to get his citizenship, and the right to work, then he struggled his way ahead, only to get smashed down by the depression. He was never rich, never had anything to speak of let alone shout about..."

Manfredo seemed to do his best to translate, but they were unconvinced. "Un traditore ... He joined the americani, fought against Italy," muttered one of the meaner men. "Contro Mussolini, " another man said. "I nazisti," still another reminded.

Manfredo explained and she insisted, "No," trying to clarify the issue, "He fought in World War I—una, no due—look at the uniform! It's from 1917, he never fought in Italy or against Italy."

But they ignored her words, inflamed by memories and passions very distant from her own. "Mussolini—We've been in hell since they killed him. At least we had something then, we had order, we had pride... Now look where we are," the meanest elder said, spitting on the hard, snow-covered stones, as Manfredo translated. "E il traductore tedesco," said his apparent sidekick, pointing to Manfredo. "Andiamo, andiamo," said Manfredo, urging the couple to follow him without a further word to the men who continued arguing, insulting, gesticulating, cursing, now oblivious to the couple and their guide who made their way out of the plaza.

2.

"We go to the house of your father's second cousin," he told her. "He's the closest relative still in the town," he explained. They climbed up the steep and narrow street past one stone house after another, passing a parade of goats seemingly without leader (though they heard a goat bell nearby); and turning to the left and right, they reached a house of stones that seemed to be built into a wall of rock that was also the side of a hill, so that the house was indeed a cave extending out toward the sidewalk. "La casa della famiglia," Manfredo announced.

He knocked on the door and a very thin and handsome young woman answered. "Lucrezia," Manfredo said. And clearly he asked to see the woman of the house whose name seemed to be Maria. The girl retreated and then returned with an older woman, very broad-beamed, in her late thirties perhaps, with round cheeks that seemed to shine without makeup and eyes that glistened with cunning and humor, all in contrast to a dress as grey as the stones and stone doorway around her. "Ah, Manfredo," she said. "Parenti" he told her. "Di sangue—la figlia di Francesco Rienza!" he explained. "Francesco...," she answered, as if she'd never heard the name. "Suo padre è cugino del padre di suo marito." "Ah!" she said, her eyes lighting up even more. "Your father is cousin of the father of her husband—he's your 3rd cousin, but Maria, she's ... his wife." All this time Maria kept her hand on her hip and a surprisingly good natured smile. "Vengono dall'America," Manfredo added, "Per dire ciao." "Ciao!" she said, shaking the husband's hand. "Ciao means goodbye, no?" asked the wife. "It also means hello," explained Manfredo, "I told her you came by to say hi." "Ah!" said the wife, "Ciao!" she said, first shaking her hand, but as their eyes met, they hugged each other." "Venite venite!" said Maria, inviting all of them into the house. "Tutti!" "A destra." And she waived them on in with enthusiasm.

Immediately they walked into a kitchen, where a large pot of something that smelled of ham and beans was steaming on a wood-burning stove. A few giant hams and cheeses were hanging from the ceiling and the smoke from the burning wood and steaming pot went up toward the hanging pieces, no doubt enriching their flavor. In the far corner of the room was an old and battered sofa, a few chairs and tables. But closer to the stove, were a few crude wooden chairs which sat around a large round table, clearly the center of social life in a space that was both kitchen and living room. It was all very dark and took the husband some moments to notice the girl who had first opened the door and then, seated at the table and eating, a chunky young man dressed in what seemed to be the uniform of a busdriver or postal worker.

Sit down, sit down, said Manfredo, translating Maria's eager and cheerful greeting, and the couple sat down, leaning their small bags against the wall. "Sono parenti di Antonio," she said. "Suoi parenti, nostri parenti!" she exclaimed and quickly moved to a cupboard bringing out glasses for all at the table and then filling them with a bottle of wine she seemed to produce from the air. "La mia sorella più piccola, Lucrezia. E io– della famiglia Coracci." "From here? From this town?" he asked Manfredo. "Di Carapella?" "Sì," Maria answered, "da quello stesso inferno!" "From the same hell," Manfredo translated. Maria and Lucrezia both laughed, the chunky young man chortled and they all laughed, now toasting, and presenting themselves, drinking down the wine and Maria immediately filling the glasses once again.

"What's one man's hell is another's heaven," rather openly flirting with Maria and reaching toward her as if he were a young lover. Maria's cheeks flushed, as she brushed his hands away. "Agh!" she grunted in feigned disgust, but was unable to hide her embarrassed pleasure at the flirting words and gestures. "He's been away from his wife too long!" she said, dismissing his advances publicly. "A week here, And now he's full of stupid words!" "Long enough to fall victim to your smile and voice," the chunky man said, continuing his flirtation. He turned out to be a postal official from Pescara who had business in the town for a few weeks and was being housed by Antonio and Maria, as it was their custom and duty to do, since Antonio was the mayor of the town. "Not the best way to repay hospitality," Manfredo said, more or less translating all that was said.

The conversation went on for several minutes, always stopping and stammering because of linguistic and other problems, with Manfredo helping things along as much as he could. It seemed that Lucrezia was paying her daily visit to help her older sister with the cooking and cleaning. Antonio had gone out to deal with some straying goats, but should be home shortly. With Manfredo's help, the wife explained that she and her husband had been traveling in Spain, which was why they could minimally communicate some things by translating from their newly won but fragile Spanish. But even before they came to Europe, the wife had promised her father that she would try to go to his hometown, to say hello to his family and to bring a handful of photos and a letter that he had given her to give them. "Fotografie!" Maria exclaimed, "Vedere, vedere!"

"No fotos! No cartas!" said the wife, shaking her head. "Just the one photo, from when he was soldier, not too many years after he left here.... We were robbed on the train," she explained, lying somewhat (they had somehow misplaced the portfolio carrying the photos, the letters, and the money her father had set aside—she blaming him, he surprised to find himself thinking that maybe she'd misplaced the bag on purpose). "We felt terrible, we almost didn't come, but I felt I had to because I'd promised my father." "O," Maria, exclaimed, clearly disappointed. "Le fotografie sono sempre belle! Che vergogna!" she added, and asked "Italiani? O siciliani?" "What?" the wife asked, not understanding the question. "She want to know if an Italian was the thief, or maybe a Sicilian." "Un calabrese," she said. "Ah! Such thieves—almost Sciliani! La stessa cosa!" Maria said. "The same thing," echoed Manfredo. But the wife understood. "Mi mamma è calabrese! That's make me half—io sono mezza—calabrese" said the wife, clearly a bit miffed. "Ma half—mezza —abruzzese, said the husband, and every one laughed, drinking more of the wine. "Viva l'Italia e tutti gli italiani!" said the official from Pescara. "E, s'intende, le belle mogli abruzzesi di Carapella del Calvizio!" he exclaimed brashly in a way that made every one laugh, some more comfortably than others, with Maria turning totally red, glistening with the words, and almost beautiful, the husband thought, in spite of her broad almost matronly peasant girth, and the stoney greyness which was beginning to frost her hair.

At that point, a gaunt man came in the door, his face at first obscured by the general darkness of the cave home and the fact that the light of the day was behind him in the doorway. "Mi hanno detto che una persona di famiglia sta qui..."

"Antonio," said Maria, her voice scaling down a tone or two, "la tua terza cugina, la figlia di Francesco Rienza con suo marito dall'America – l'America!"

"Figlio de Lorenzo. Francesco, ah," Antonio said, seating himself ever so slowly at the table, with a nod to the chunky postal official. "Il tuo lavoro, finito?" he asked gruffly. "Cosi, cosi" signalled the official, almost touching thumb and forefinger together. "...Oggi ... domani" he added, shrugging his shoulders, and squinting at Antonio as if to leave all in doubt, before taking another drink.

"Francesco Rienza…" Antonio repeated, with a tired voice that matched his movements. He seemed to be thinking back slowly to times when perhaps he had thought more quickly, filled more then than now with the springy hope of youthful dreams. Clearly he was many years older than Maria, but he seemed old beyond age, grey and worn like the streets of the town. Maria poured him some wine, but he seemed somewhat irritated, if you could so characterize the actions of one who seemed so lethargic in his movements and expressions. Perhaps it was the simulation of what he knew to be the proper reaction. "Ma perché non hai servito niente?" he asked, and Maria now responded with force. "Perché tu come uomo e parente suo…" "She's says that he's the one who should welcome you to his house and offer you something to eat," explained Manfredo, as Antonio nodded. "Avete anche ragione," he said, acquiescing. "Ma we are not hungry non possiamo quedar—restare multo tiempo,"she said. "We can't stay here long—just one night," she said, "we just came to say hello and share some pictures and words…" "Well, that was the original idea," said the husband. Manfredo translated, but it was all too late. Maria and Lucrezia started ladling bowls of bean and pasta soup, clearly mixed with the ceiling ham and cheese. They sliced up some crude bread with a pairing knife and served it around. "You don't have to do this," said the husband, "we only came to say hello." Manfredo translated, and Antonio said, "But you cannot say hello and goodbye, there is no hotel here and this is your home in Carapella." "No," said the wife, "we wouldn't think—" "It's a duty and honor to serve the family of my great uncle," Antonio intervened. "You are welcome in my house. You are welcome to stay here tonight and as many nights as you may wish or may be able to stay," he said, but not with the spirit of a proud patriarch upholding family traditions but with that strange, atonal fatigue in a voice that only joined life by rote. Manfredo translated all, and, understanding, the couple made their second protest, but Antonio interrupted. "It's settled," he said, and then filled his glass and toasted. "Salute," he said, filling his glass and toasting. And "mangiate, mangiate."

They sat at the table eating and speaking haltingly, Antonio saying little but seeming to listen as Manfredo and Maria took the lead in questioning the wife and sometimes the husband, with Lucrezia saying practically nothing but even the postal official piping in from time to time—and with Manfredo translating all as best he could.

"My Father always told me about the cold here, but he also spoke of good food, capra, ham, cheese, wine. He told me the family was very poor and that he worked for the local priest, cleaning, setting up and taking down —cose di cerimonia. He told me something happened with the priest, that they had words and the priest was furious and began to throw rocks at him. So he left swearing he would never come back. He never did." He went to New York, she explained, but returned to Europe to fight in World War I and win his citizenship; and on his return went to Cleveland, where he worked twenty-years as a streetcar conductor, married her mother, who was from a Calabrese coal-mining family in Pennsylvania, had gotten a normal school education and become a teacher, but, heeding her mother and her biological clock, left it all behind to become a working class wife and, much later, in mid-depression, a mother, the couple moving eventually to Los Angeles, where they bought a home and the father worked as a carpenter. She, the daughter born to them late in their life, had gone to college, studied and was now a social worker, though what she liked most was to write stories of adventures. "What kind of adventures?" Maria asked, fascinated. "Wouldn't you like to know," said the wife, giving Maria a wink, as they both broke into laughter, bonding somehow across vast differences. "Amore, amore," said the postal official, "that's what women mean when they speak of adventures and stories."

"But you are the only child?" Antonio asked finally. "No I have a younger brother, born even later to them—Francesco or Frank." "A son!" Maria chortled, "And what does he look like? you don't have any pictures?" "See?" said the postal authority. "She wants to see the good-looking brother!" "The calabrese stole her pictures," Lucrezia said. "Well I don't really know who stole them," the wife corrected, "it happened in Calabria—that much is for sure. I had photos and a letter, and some money, but they stole everything. But yes, I do have the picture of my father when he was an American soldier," she said, taking out the photo a second time that day and now passing around the faded print, showing the hard faced son of Lorenzo Rienza some 45 years before, a young man perhaps not too different from the way he looked when he left the town. "You know, I have a picture too," said the husband, suddenly remembering—"of the whole family, at Christmas last year." And he took a picture from his wallet. "See, there we are with her father and mother, and also my brother-in-law Frank and his wife." "Ah, there he is an old man," said Maria. "But the brother's young, good-looking Abruzzi boy," "Half Calabrian," said the wife. "Good looking Italian boy with his goodlooking wife," said Maria, staring at the picture. "But it's the daughter, not the son who visits us," she added. "Mala sorte sua," said the postal official, chortling again. "America is a strange and wonderful country," she continued, "con brave figlie who come to visit." "To America," said Manfredo, and they drank another glass.

"And how long you married?" Maria asked and Manfredo translated. "Due anni," said the husband. "And no children yet?" "No," he answered, "but we're working at it," he lied. Manfredo interpreted and every one laughed. "You can continue your work here in Carapella," he said. And every one laughed, except the wife, who then asked, "And what about you, Maria?" What about the family? "Here we are," Manfredo started. "We lived through the first war, and then came Mussolini, and then the Nazis and the Russians and the Americans." "People born, people die," said Maria. "Many went to America or just the city—to Roma to find work." "My brother is in Rome," said Antonio. "He has become an insurance man, an administrator," he clarified. "I mean, he doesn't sell, he administers something. My father and mother are there helping with the children, preparing the food." "They wash clothes in a machine, watch TV at night, and drive around in the family car," said Maria. "They are very far from us now, though they visit once in awhile. We're the ones who're stuck in this godforsaken pile of rocks, keeping the property, waiting for the town to die and us with it." "And you don't have any children?" the wife asked. "Two," she said, "the boy is in Rome with his brother, but our girl Antonio went and sent to the convent," she said almost shouting. "The convent," the husband murmured, "but was she very religious?"

"She was very hungry," said Antonio, now standing up as if too much had been said and it was enough at least for now. "We are happy to meet you here, and learn of Francesco Rienza, and meet his daughter and husband. We hope one day Francesco and his wife and his son will also come, and that we will see each other before we all die." But now I must go. Manfredo and I will take you to the house where your father was born and lived and then to the square. There is not much to see in Carapella del Calvzio, but you should see it all. I will leave you in the square, but Manfredo will take you around and then back here—yes Manfredo?" "Right," said Manfredo, translating everything Antonio said. "It's not that he has such a busy schedule in this bustling town, it's not that there are visitors to cab around every minute or every day" the visiting official chimed in. "I for one need to finish my official work and prepare to get back to Pescara by tomorrow night at the latest." "Just one day more, almost like us," said the wife "So," said Antonio, seeming to ignore all this. "We will see you around, Manfredo will take you back, and in the meantime, Maria and Lucrezia will prepare something for dinner and a bed for you to sleep tonight."

3.

They took the couple up one path and down another, passing cave-houses and then a group of fully structured buildings not set against or in a hill. The cold began to penetrate very quickly and the coupled buttoned up exhaling clouds of smoke from their mouths into the chilling air, as they passed only an occasional person, and more often, a dog and then a small herd of goats that went briskly by. "Americani?" the goatherd asked Antonio, "Sì," he nodded, "sono parenti in visita," he answered, a bit more robust sounding as he spoke to a neighbor. ""Eccolo qui," he said finally, indicating a two-storey hovel identical in so many ways to the other ones they'd passed. "You take pictures, no? This a good place to start, no?" said Manfredo. "Yes, you take pictures to my father's second cousin," Antonio suggested. And the husband took pictures of his wife between Manfredo and Antonio standing in front of the house where his father-in-law had been born and spent the first years of his life.

Then Antonio unlocked a padlock on the front door, and walked in. "No one living here now?" the wife asked. "No," said Manfredo, "Abbandonata," he said for many years now. "It is legally mine now, "Antonio said, "but you are welcome to live here." "It's not possible," she said. "I have my work in America now." "America very nice," said Manfredo, "above all California…. Maybe we come visit you sometime and see movie stars," he added. "Yes," wisecracked the husband, "You can come and meet all the Italian beauties who live there now." But it was clear to the husband that they all knew that reciprocal visits were probably not in the cards. "In any event, you should take your pictures to show Francesco Rienza," Antonio added.

Dutifully the husband got out his cheap Kodak camera and took a picture of his three companions in front of the house. They then took their tour, going through the living room and kitchen, then climbing the stairs to the two bedrooms—a master bedroom where her father's parents probably slept and where he was probably conceived on a cold winter night, and then finally to the second bedroom that was probably (though none of them would know for sure) the room where Francesco Rienza and his brothers and sisters slept. They took a couple of photos, but the flash failed and the pictures would probably be too dark. Then the husband took some through the windows, imagining his father-in-law as a boy staring out at the rocks and the falling snow, the goats and the relentless sky as he dreamed whatever dreams he dreamed in this small house in the small mountain town he would leave at fourteen and never (or probably never) return to except by proxy.

Then it was down the stairs, and then down the hill, making their way as quickly as they could toward the town square, and now they were standing again near the small cathedral, clearly the center of the old life and ways that were dying as the days went by. Here Antonio excused himself to take care of pressing obligations, and the couple made their way with Manfredo, past the few townspeople still remaining as this day edged on, nodding but not speaking this time as they walked toward the cathedral and stood in its shadow—a small squat church which no Gothic pretensions never meant to serve any but a small congregation. "Here your father worshipped and worked, right?" said Manfredo, "and then had his fight with the priest." "Yes," said the wife. "And you know why?" "Well he always made me think it was something over religion or maybe politics, but I don't know" "Yes," said Manfredo, "It maybe was something else. He was very bad priest, he became a true Mussolini priest, but the rumor was he abused the boys, and it was not just hitting them.' "Is that true?" she asked. "it never dawned on me." "That is what is said. I can only tell you when he died and they gave him last rites, some one desecrated the body most obscenely, dumping how you say … human shit on the body." "My god," said the husband. "No wonder he left, no wonder he hated the church with such a passion and became a protestant." "Became a protestant!" Manfredo expressed shock. "The priests can do many wrong things, but you should not become a protestant." "But what you say would explain many things, maybe," said the wife "—including why he's such a machista," "Machista?" asked Manfredo, apparently not familiar with the Spanish word, "Uno che fa stare zitte le donne?" "Yes—a man who puts women down," she said—"or makes them open up," she added. "Ah," he said, clearly taken aback. "And maybe that's why I'm here and not him and not my brother." "You are perhaps your father's son more than your brother," said Manfredo, the husband nodding his head in surprise at this insight.

With that, they entered the simple church they called cathedral. They looked down the rows of benches to the altar, then moved around the church to look at the few drab pictures and relics, mainly bones and broken objects of wood, the broken but never very impressive stained glass window, the benches themselves, and then the image of the crucified Christ and a saint. "The saint is San Pancrazio," said Manfredo. "The town's patron saint." "We are proud of this image and that of the Christ which you can see are not very bad church sculptures for a town like this." "But who did them?" the husband asked. "A man, Bartoldo, I think it was, who worked in the church many years ago. Indeed in your father's time…" "Yes," said the wife, "I think I remember him saying that part of his work was with a sculptor or artist, he was a kind of apprentice, which maybe is why he wound up being a carpenter." "Well. Bartoldo you can see was no master, but he wasn't so bad for some one who never had training and lived all his early years here; he had the passion. And the rebel flair," said Manfredo, pointing now to the Christ, whose loin cloth did not seem (was it really so? the husband asked himself) to quite hide one of his testicles.

"Every one said he was crazy, and of course it's always the crazy ones who end up being the town artists. The crazy ones and the drunks, and that was him too, all right. He ended up a total drunk, until no one wanted him around any more. They kind of pushed him out of town." "Where did he go? How did he end up?" "No one knows," Manfredo told them, "it's just that he went off many years ago, and some people were very upset saying others had forced Bartoldo out, and it wasn't right given the good sculptures he did. And then when the priest died, the rumor spread that one of his worst victims was Bartoldo. Which is maybe why he drank as much as he did and maybe also why his work is as good as it is." "Or as bad," said the wife. "Your father carves in his small way too," the husband said. "A frustrated artist, maybe." "Yes, like your father at the piano. … And you with those stories you write without any imagination. Maybe you'll even try to make this into a story." "Or maybe you will," he said. "Small petty artists, all of us." she said. "Big illusions, but nothing much to say. Except maybe my father did have something—maybe he and Bartholdo had more in common than the priest. Maybe there was something between them," she said, laughing at her own witty suggestion. The husband glared at her. "So now you have your little story," he said. "And maybe you have yours.," she retorted. "To create you have to destroy," she added. "But I don't think you have it in you."

Manfredo perhaps pretended not to hear, but led them out of the church, waited as the husband took his photos of church and square, and then escorted them across the square, where just two old men sat, nodding to them as they passed. The husband heard one say "Americani" and had the distinct impression that the other spat at the ground.

4.

On their way to the house, the husband asked where they might find a store, because he wanted to buy something for the house. "But the few places we have to buy are closed by now," Manfredo said, "And Antonio's house is a store too, you know, where people buy some bread or cheese or wine or goatmeat—or even pasta when Maria and Lucrezia get the urge to make some. But they won't think of letting you buy there. You are their guest now, for you the time for buying gifts is past."

Very shortly thereafter, they entered the house, where the postal official and Maria seemed lost in conversation, laughing and joking, with a patter of innuendo, all the chores seemed to fall on Lucrezia. "And have you seen our beautiful town?" Maria asked. "The gem of the Abruzzi," said the chunky official from Pescara. "Yes," said the husband, "seen the house of Francesco and the cathedral, seen much, but the cold is unbearable," he said. "And the rocks are rocks."

"The rocks are rocks," said the official, seemingly drunk with the phrase. "Like the heart of l'innamorata as she scourns the poet soul of the man in love," he said falling to his knees in mock confession of eternal love. "I ssassi ce li ha nella testa," Maria said, laughing at the fool at her feet. "She says the rocks are in his head and it's time to finish cooking the dinner and not think of stupid things."

But thinking she is, thought the husband, a bit aroused himself over the very plump peasant woman living her drab life in her dress as grey as the walls and her heart suddenly tripping light, it seemed, as she encouraged expressions of love, desire and devotion she had to know were entirely false.

Lucrezia and she went their way to cook the dinner, while the postal official stayed in his place and Manfredo showed the husband and wife around the house. Soon Maria joined them, with pictures she had. "I asked my mother," she explained. "She said we too are distant cousins."

"How wonderful!" said the wife. "Then we're almost sisters!" They laughed together, and Maria produced an album. "She asked me to show you some family pictures so you'd know about us," she said, and the two sat together as she showed the wife the pictures and explained them one by one. Meanwhile the husband and Manfredo talked about the war, about Nazis and Communists, while the postal official, eager to finish the work he was sent to do, dozed off to sleep and Lucrezia kept preparing the dinner. Later in the evening, Antonio returned, and dinner was served. They all came together at the table underneath the meats and cheeses. Wine and words of welcome flowed again, as the night drew on and the cold Abruzzi wind kicked up its heels.

Soon they were devouring their food, talking as best they could. Maria even produced a radio to play as they talked, and the wife even tried the sad apple pie joke her father'd told her—that when he first came to the U.S. he didn't know what to order, so another immigrant said, just tell them, "Apple-a-pie an a cupa coffee." So he did that and always got served apple pie and coffee. But he got tired of it and one day asked how he could ask for a hamburger with French fries. So when the waitress came, he tried to tell her, gimme a—a… a—apple-a-pie an a cupa coffee." Every one around the table tried to laugh, though it wasn't clear they'd gotten the joke. First one, then another laughed but it didn't last long. Then wife told them, "He always named everything on the table before we ate. Maybe it was like praying, or maybe showing how far he'd come from those apple pie days. He was always proud of what he'd done and when my mother fixed a great Italian meal, and we said, "it's great mom!,' he'd bring his hands down on the table—only now they were fists—like this," said the wife banging her closed fists down on the table so that the wine swirled in the glasses and one almost fell over. "Damn right, it's good," she said, apparently imitating his low, Italian-accented voice, and "look who bought it." Every one laughed again, and Maria lifted her glass, "Salute a Francesco Rienza e alla sua figlia americana," she cried out, and everyone toasted, drank and laughed. But it was almost night—time to sleep, Antonio and the postal official already with eyes half-closed, almost asleep from too much wine and talk it was difficult to follow. Manfredo said goodnight softly and left, while Maria and Lucrezia heated some coals and then led the couple into a room of their own to spend the night.

"Here's where you'll sleep," said Maria. "But you must know how," she said, laughing. First the two sisters brought out a wooden cradle which they put under a large down blanket. Then they put the coals they'd been heating and set them in an open brazier and then, shocking him, set the open brazier on the cradle and covered the cradle with the blanket. "But won't this burn?" asked the husband. "No, nothing will burn but your privates!" said Maria laughing loudly and returning them to the kitchen, where they sat around the open stove and radio waiting for the bed to warm, the men now having retired, and the radio now playing a song they'd heard so often in the south and in Rome that they thought it a current hit: "Volare, ohohohoh, cantare, ohohohoh." "Francesco Rienza vola in America dove mangia apple pie e noi qui a Carapella con il blu di pinto di blu!" Maria exclaimed, almost sobbing, the wife now taking her hand.

Minutes later, she returned with them to the bedroom, to remove the burning brazier and urge them to now get undressed and get under the covers. "Maybe tonight, here, you'll do what you haven't been able to do, and another Francesco Rienza will be conceived in this wonderful mountain town!" she said, gesturing and mimicking until they understood, laughing and hugging the wife. "It will get cold by six," she said, "but by then things should have been pretty hot!":

The two were finally alone, not undressing but adding sweaters to their night attire, then plunging into the hot blanket, embracing tightly more from the cold than from something burning inside. "Make love to me," she said hoarsely, "Make me come." He eased her out of pants, opened his, and started to mount her. "No," she said, "not like that. Do it the way I taught you, the way I like it," she urged. So he first moistened his middle finger in his mouth and then in her vagina, but then removed it, entering her there now with his forefinger while he pressed his thumb against her clitoris, and gradually pushed the lubed middle finger into her nether opening, while she raised her leg over his elbow, pushing down and virtually locking down on his wrist and occupied fingers, pressing down over his arm, he feeling his finger and, yes his finger nail digging into the edge of her hardened stool, she pressing down, pressing down, rocking his arm with her leg until she writhed into an orgasm based on friction and who knows what fantasy, he waiting his turn until she said, "yes, yes, now you can fuck me, fuck me here in Italy, Abruzzi, my town, where my grandfather fucked my grandmother till my father was born, and my father fucked my mother till I was born, and I fucked you and Maria and every one until god, oh god!" And she came again, he now along with her—though in the precise moment, she pushed him out, grabbing him so that he finished in her hand. "There, there," she sighed, "but no seed—nothing of that," he panting with a deep frustration in the heated sheets, staving off the night of cold that came on them fully only after they were long exhausted and asleep.

5.

The cold woke him in the morning, only to find she had gone from the room, he washing quickly in freezing water, cleaning his whole body, but above all his fingers. He entered the common room and found her at the table with Maria, joking and laughing as if they'd formed some kind of womanly pact that kept men off limits. He and Antonio came in simultaneously and were instantly invited for coffee and large crackers meant for dipping. Manfredo came in the door just as the Pescara official made his way into the common room, and the cast very quickly became complete as Lucrezia came in the door.

And then the American's wife surprised him. "I'm glad you're all here because I can thank you all for your hospitality, and tell you that we have to go this morning," she quickly told the group, Manfredo translating. It seemed she had purposely not consulted her departure plans with him ahead of time, so all he could was improvise. "We have things to do in Rome that can't wait. It's been wonderful getting to know you, and I hope we can keep in touch and see each other again."

"I was hoping we could stay another day," said the wife. "It's so terrible to leave when we've just come, but it was just a first visit." She said, lying to herself perhaps, or them. "It was great to meet you and great to find a new cugina"! said Maria, "And who knows, maybe a new bambino!" she laughed beaming broadly, giving the wife a hug. "It has been my pleasure to meet the daughter of Francesco Rienza and to know what happened to his life," said Antonio in his listless tone like a man who has ceased living even as he continues to walk, talk and breathe. "I want you to have the two pictures we showed you yesterday, the only ones we could bring," said the wife, taking the one she had in her purse while he drew his from his wallet. "We wish we could offer you more." "No, you have offered more than it was necessary," said Antonio. "We have some pictures for you to take to your father. And I will give you the telephone number of my brother in Roma. We'll call him, so he knows that you are coming to stay with him in his apartment with my parents and his wife and children—and our son." They could do nothing but take the pictures and then the names and phone numbers. "I will take you to L'Aquila," said Manfredo. "No, it's not necessary, we can go back as we came." "No," said Antonio. "Manfredo will take you to L'Aquila. It is no bother." "And you, Antonio?" the wife said. "Shouldn't you take us too?" "Yes," said Maria quickly, "Manfredo can do his job, but you—you're supposed to go too." "Well, you can go with us," said Antonio, "And we can visit Anna on the way home." "No, no, non posso," Maria answered, "There's too much to straighten out here and Lucrezia can't stay to help today." Lucrezia looked down, and Antonio frowned, but went on. "And you?" he addressed the official, who quickly declared his need to stay longer. "Molto lavoro da fare," he said, "things to do." He couldn't leave until the afternoon or maybe even the next day. "Ah," said Antonio. The die were cast. "Then it's best that we go now so you can catch the bus to Rome and we call my brother from L'Aquila before I visit Anna."

The couple gathered their things and went outside, hugging Maria and Lucrezia. The husband grouped them for a picture, and then Lucrezia took the camera so he could join the group for a final shot. The wife whispered something to Maria that made her blush and laugh, they both laughed out loud, Maria hugging the wife especially hard, and then letting her make her way into Manfredo's van, as Antonio climbed into the front passenger seat. The couple waved goodbye as the van made its way down the hill to the center of the town, passing the cathedral and a few men, probably the same regulars from yesterday, standing around the plaza. They waved toward the men, who seemed to return the friendly salute with indifference, though one gestured toward them by raising his fist.

"They're probably calling us traitors," said the husband. Neither Antonio nor Manfredo said a word, staring ahead, but as they passed the town gate, Manfredo said, "you don't have to go, I can take them." "Andiamo, andiamo," said Antonio, his voice especially tired and hollow. They proceeded on the road down the hill arriving finally at the highway. The husband looked up at the tall rock-built, cross-topped building across the highway from the town road. "What is that building?" he asked. "That's the convent," Antonio said, "Where Anna my daughter is." "It looks like a hard life there." "Yes," he agreed, "La vita è dura" "Si," the husband said, terribly sad and angry, but unable to think of anything else to say. The four people were mainly silent all the way to L'Aquila, where Manfredo took them to the depot where they should not have to wait long for the bus that would take them to Rome. They said goodbye again, going through some mindless ritual, Antonio stiff, but correct, Manfredo now cold and formal, the husband sadder and angrier than ever. As they made their last goodbyes, the wife handed something to Manfredo. "No," he protested taken aback. "You spent a lot, you helped us," she said. And he suddenly stopped, "Very well," he said, "For services and expenses," he said, winter in his voice, and returning to the driver's seat without a further word or gesture. And then the van was gone.

6.

They made no effort to enter the depot; instead, she insisted they take a cab to the inn where they had stayed before, checking in and going directly to their room.

"We found out too much, saw too much, and your last moves were beyond words," said the husband settling onto the bed.

"You're upset about a passing moment," said his wife, lying down next to him.

"They may never be the same."

"Well maybe that's good."

"Who are we to decide that, like gods who call on a couple and change all."

"You worry too much."

"You all but set it up, you did it on purpose, as if you came here to do them in."

"My name is Vengeance," she laughed.

"Yes, that's right. It's like you came here to avenge your father against his relatives and town. You wanted your father's cousin to be betrayed. And worse, you came to avenge yourself against your father too by tearing up his family all the more."

"Maybe you're right," she admitted, "Maybe I paid him back for pulling my mother out of her little career, making her a victim of his Abruzzi machismo—or whatever," she said, "and trying to make me his victim too."

"Well, he failed on that count," he said. "Or maybe he didn't. But you got yours back, didn't you?"

"I'm my mother's daughter. A witch from the south of Calabria—almost Sicilia, paying back for what they took from me!" she laughed. "And I'm also Modern Woman, breaking up the world! ... But all this is nonsense. The simple fact is we gave a sad peasant woman a chance for a happy afternoon in a hard life."

"It's not that simple," he said. "You didn't want her to be happy as much as you wanted Antonio to be betrayed. You didn't care about her enjoying that nasty Pescara bureaucrat, you wanted to imagine his pleasure having her."

"Maybe you're right, " she said, insinuating her tongue into his ear, and reaching for him. "Maybe I wanted to betray Antonio, just as I want to betray you. There's always something to pay back any way, like sending the girl to a convent when you send the poor little boy off to Rome."

"He didn't create the system, he's just played out the options he had, making the hard decisions he had to make—like taking us to L'Aquila."

"Well, I can't live that way, I reject it completely. I want to be able to do whatever with whoever and whenever I want," she said, rubbing him, bringing him to erection in spite of himself. And it was true, this is how she was, her ruthless will to realize her desires no matter what the cost.

"But don't think you're so innocent in all this," she continued, caressing him, almost mocking him "—as if you didn't play your part. You probably wanted to have her too but just in your mind, so you went along.. You could've stopped Antonio from taking us."

"You knew the logic of it all, you said it, and Maria just had to confirm it. You set him up."

"All he had to do was refuse. But no, he was too dead and stupid, with all his sense of duty."

"Maybe that's why he's the mayor."

"Well, everything depends on how you look at it all, doesn't it? Looks to me like the whole thing could be seen as your fault."

And he suddenly thought that maybe she was right, thinking that it was surely his fault for being with her, for putting up with her and following along in her maddest moments, for allowing her to manipulate his persistent desire. His member was now persistent and hard as she continued to rub him, breath and tongue his ear. He looked at her lovely olive face, her, full sensuous lips, her wonderful shoulders and found her terrible and beautiful. He knew he had to find the strength to overcome his feelings. But that would be later, some other day or year. In the meantime he accepted the fact that he'd collaborated in a kind of treason that might change the life of a couple, and the life of the couple he was still a part of as well.

"I don't see what business it is of yours any way, this was my family, my story." She said, pushing his fingers against her clitoris and pressing down on his hand. "Why don't you go to Russia or Rumania and look for your family's stories. Why do you have to live through me and judge me?"

"Maybe you're right," he conceded, "you're probably right," he said on his back, letting her straddle his pelvis and begin to honker down, even as he realized that her suggestion was bogus, since she must know that he and "his people" had very little nostalgia for the old countries where they were such outsiders and where, besides, most of those who'd stayed had probably been murdered. But he let that pass. Instead, he gave into her urges, as her fingers moved down his back, one of them insinuating into his nether zone. "I'll tell you one thing," he managed to say in half-hearted defiance, "I might go, but I probably wouldn't take you."

"That's fine with me," she said, digging in deeper. "Who'd want to visit your old miserable places where your family and people suffered so terribly, poor boy—and you were all so innocent and undeserving of malice and bad treatment," she continued, almost chanting, as her finger entered fully now, and as he tried to resist a last time. "No," he said. "Sì," she whispered, "Sì," she said, probing deeper and accepting his now full erection, which seemed to grow and quiver the more outrageous her words or actions. "What does any of it matter anyway?" she quipped, poised for a final offensive. "Who cares! We both got our stories, and we'll probably never go there again. We might not even visit the family in Rome, and even if we do, we'll probably never know what happened in that town after we left, right?"

"Right," he agreed, ever so sadly, even as she began thrusting at him and probing him with a violent insistence he couldn't resist. "We'll probably never know."

And they never did.

About the Author

Chair of Modern and Classical Languages at the University of Houston, Marc Zimmerman is Professor Emeritus of Latin American and Latino Studies at the University of Illinois at Chicago. He holds a Ph.D. in Comparative Literature from the University of California, San Diego and an M.A. in Creative Writing (Language Arts) from San Francisco State University, where he studied with Walter Van Tilburg Clark, Mark Harris, Herbert Wilner and Ray West.

Some of his plays have been produced, including his adaptation of Kafka's "A Hunger Artist," which won a national playwriting contest and was presented by the Comedia Players of Menlo Park, California in 1963. Working on African American thematics, he wrote *Clues for Tomorrow* in 1963 and adapted George Büchner's *Woyzeck* in 1967. A short play and stories of his (including "Valentine's Day 1947" and "The Landlord") have appeared in *The Dartmouth Quarterly, Descant* and *The Great River Review*. "The Univited" is scheduled to appear in an Italian translation, "I non invitati," by Alessandro Carrera in the journal, *Nuova prosa*, published in Milan by Edizioni Greco & Greco.

By himself and with others, Zimmerman has written and edited *The Central American Quartet* (1980-96); *Processes of Caribbean Societies: Ideologies and Literatures* (1983), *Lucien Goldmann: El estructuralismo genético y la creación cultural* (1985); *Literature and Politics in the Central American Revolutions* (1990); *U.S. Latino Literature* (1992); *Literature and Resistance in Guatemala* (1995); *New World [Dis]Orders* (1998); *Globalización, nación y (post)modernidad: Estudios culturales puertorriqueños* (2001); *Las ciudades latinoamericanas en el nuevo [des]orden mundial* (2004)*; Estudios culturales y cuestiones de globales* (2005); and a whole series of books, *Pre-Post and Post-Positions* (Global CASA/LACASA and Bravo y Allende 2005-6). Zimmerman worked with migrant farm workers in Minnesota; he served in the Sandinista Ministry of Culture; he has also taught at San Diego State U., the U. of Michigan at Ann Arbor, McGill University, the Universidad Autónoma de Nicaragua (Managua) and the Universidad de Puerto Rico (Río Piedras). He is the director of Global CASA and LACASA Publications.